Babaru

ILLINOIS SHORT FICTION

Crossings by Stephen Minot
A Season for Unnatural Causes by Philip F. O'Connor
Curving Road by John Stewart
Such Waltzing Was Not Easy by Gordon Weaver

Rolling All the Time by James Ballard
Love in the Winter by Daniel Curley
To Byzantium by Andrew Fetler
Small Moments by Nancy Huddleston Packer

One More River by Lester Goldberg
The Tennis Player by Kent Nelson
A Horse of Another Color by Carolyn Osborn
The Pleasures of Manhood by Robley Wilson, Jr.

The New World by Russell Banks
The Actes and Monuments by John William Corrington
Virginia Reels by William Hoffman
Up Where I Used to Live by Max Schott

The Return of Service by Jonathan Baumbach
On the Edge of the Desert by Gladys Swan
Surviving Adverse Seasons by Barry Targan
The Gasoline Wars by Jean Thompson

Desirable Aliens by John Bovey
Naming Things by H. E. Francis
Transports and Disgraces by Robert Henson
The Calling by Mary Gray Hughes

Into the Wind by Robert Henderson
Breaking and Entering by Peter Makuck
The Four Corners of the House by Abraham Rothberg
Ladies Who Knit for a Living by Anthony E. Stockanes

Pastorale by Susan Engberg
Home Fires by David Long
The Canyons of Grace by Levi Peterson
Babaru by B. Wongar

BABARU

Stories by

B. Wongar

UNIVERSITY OF ILLINOIS PRESS

Urbana Chicago London

Publication of this work was supported in part by grants from the National Endowment for the Arts and the Illinois Arts Council, a state agency.

Manufactured in the United States of America

"Wawa, My Brother" and "Warand, the Dingo" first appeared in *Ethnic Australia* (Brisbane: Phoenix Publications, 1981) and "Balandja, the Cockatoos" in *South Pacific Stories* (Brisbane: SPACLALS, 1980).

The rock paintings used as illustrations in this volume are reproduced from *Australian Aboriginal Paintings in Western and Central Arnhem Land,* by E J. Brandl (Canberra: Australian Institute of Aboriginal Studies, 1973) and are reprinted by permission.

Library of Congress Cataloging in Publication Data

Wongar, B.
Babaru: stories.

(Illinois short fiction)
Contents: Kury, the wife—Wawa, my brother—Cockatoo man—[etc.]
I. Title. II. Series.
PR9619.3.W62B3 1982 823 82-4860
ISBN 0-252-00995-9 (cloth) AACR2
ISBN 0-252-00996-7 (paper)

To Alan Paton

You taught me that all men should be equal.

Contents

I'm taking you to bare and waterless country.

—wailing chant, northern Australia

Kury, the Wife

It should not be far away now—Nura, my tribal country. Beyond the last clumps of spinifex and the wide stretch of dry land, Yapu, the mountain, should soon show itself, looking at first as if it is floating on the afternoon haze and seeming to be part of both the sky and the land. Once you reach there, however, and climb to the topmost rock, every detail of the surroundings can be seen as clearly as the palm of your hand.

I wonder if the dingo knows we are getting close; he seems in no hurry today. His three legs all seem to be failing him, and when he staggers particularly badly he sits on the sand shivering and jerking his head as if urging me to turn back. We are both old, and perhaps we are not as sprightly as before, but there is nothing here to harm us now—the whites have gone for good. The night before last Niyari—the Boss—called to see me in my dreams: "Here," he said, "have your bloody bush back—I am off to my own world."

No, I will not be there today, but perhaps tomorrow. It takes more than two camps for even a younger hunter to cross the wasteland. Even the wind and the spirits have to struggle when traveling around here, and for me and Pupa—whom life has worn out—the journey is a slow and hard one.

We may not have to go all the way, though, for Tiwa might have left the homestead and be heading this way. She is my *kury,* my wife, who should be with me, and now that Niyari has gone we can be together again. It should not take Tiwa long to get here, and if she has already crossed the mountain she might appear from behind the clumps of spinifex at the end of this very day, if not before. When you are young you can move so fast that only the spirits or the wind are swifter.

I will sit down there under that grass tree and let poor Pupa catch up with me. The day is still very hot, even though the sun is quite low, so maybe I should rest in the shade and wait for the evening cool before pressing on farther. The whites wear hats to shield them from the hot sun. The Boss had one with a wide brim and a cord slung beneath his jaws to keep the thing on his head even during a windstorm. I never saw him out without it, ever since he came to Nura, but perhaps he took it off at night—Tiwa could tell about that but I have never asked.

At first we did not mind having Niyari and his herd of cattle about. The beasts did no harm to our people, but they did trample all over the country and I suppose that made the spirits unhappy, for no rain came for years and the land grew dry and bare. Windstorms pranced about now and then, blowing clouds of dust from one side of the sky to the other, but they brought good to no one—they only showed the anger of our spirits.

Well, Pupa has found us some tucker; it's a blue-tongued lizard that the dog carries in his mouth like a stick and lays in front of me before flinging himself down in the shade with his tongue hanging out, struggling for breath. It's a pity that the dingo has only three legs, and so cannot run down any larger animals, but he often sniffs about and finds reptiles, and sometimes he leads me into the spinifex to a clutch of emu eggs.

It is water though, not food, that we worry most about, for there's not much of it to be seen around here. The country looks dusty and worn out by what must have been a long dry spell, though I cannot tell exactly how long since it rained. Perhaps this drought is to be even tougher than the last one years ago, and that might be why Niyari has left. The white man must be afraid that neither he nor his beasts could survive another such ordeal. During the last drought he dug great holes and furrowed the ground with long channels to trap every drop of water from the smallest shower of rain, but in spite of his efforts only dust clouds gathered overhead.

The sun is about to sink into the mist at the fringe of the sky.

Yapu shows much more clearly with rosy light splashed over the bare rocks; we must hurry to get closer to it now, for the shadows are lengthening and darkness will soon set in.

Tiwa will be making her campfire now, so I must be on the lookout for rising smoke—I should be able to see it even if it's at the foot of the mountain. Tiwa will have a bag full of water—she would never set out on a journey without it, for she has lived in the homestead for many years and has learned a lot of the white man's way. The Boss always carried a water bag in the bush, though it had not helped him much that time, during the long drought, when I found him lying in the scrub near the creek. His precious bag was long empty and the man's mouth was as dry and stiff as the canvas. No sound would come from his cracked lips. I dug in the creek bed until I found a frog buried in the sand, and though its belly was only half full of water, that was enough to bring Niyari back from death.

The creek springs from the foot of the hills on the other side of the mountain, runs through scrub country past a small rise where the whites have now built a homestead, and then through a broad plain toward the horizon and the lake far beyond Nura. I have never been there, but the spirits travel that way every night to fill their *piti,* their wooden dishes, and carry the water back to the mountain. You can see, every night, the path they take across the middle of the sky. Such a track they leave—every black fellow must be there, I reckon, ferrying water. Some of the water spills out of the *piti* sometimes, but it sinks very quickly into the sandy bed of the creek.

The whites call that track the Milky Way and most say that they don't believe anything about our *munga,* our spirit world—but Niyari took my word for it and sank a bore on the creek bank, halfway between the homestead and the mountain. Whenever there was wind enough to spin the tin wheel he built, enough to keep the thing rattling for a while, then water would come gushing out from the end of the pipe. Niyari believed all right—after that.

Pupa is clawing at me again, staring into my face and making whining noises, though his mouth is hardly open. He's cursing me for something, I'm sure, for the dingo has a mind like a human, and though he can make no words, he has feelings just the same as we do. Perhaps Pupa wants to remind me that I have made no fire and he has never known a camp without it; but I am too worn out to gather wood, and anyway, what good would it serve when I feel too weak to struggle with the firesticks and made the first spark. Now if Tiwa were only here—it would take just a moment or two for her to set up camp and raise the first smoke: she is so good at it. Young women are given to old men, to take care of us, and with one like Tiwa about, life would certainly make a turn for the better, for me and old Pupa.

The dingo howls. I wonder why he is not asleep; perhaps it is thirst that keeps the poor animal awake. It's good that we are so close to the mountain now, for among the rocks there should be some bush berries—a handful of those will kill our thirst for a while—and juicy wild figs grow among the boulders too. There might not be much tucker after such a long drought, but if you scrape the ground, and know where to look, a few bulbs hiding there in the soil may turn up. Those, crushed . . . or anything else to yield a drop or two of water will do us both good.

The sun has risen a spear high now, and the boulders are warming up fast. I must hurry up the slopes and reach the top of the mountain before the rocks underfoot become like red coals. The dingo lags behind, sitting down now and then as if hoping that I will turn back, but rising again as I move and struggling forward. It must be torture to climb as he does with one leg missing, but he makes it somehow. I have tried to help him over some of the bigger boulders, but whenever I reach down, Pupa backs away so as not to be caught. It seems that he is not thirsty, for when I crushed some gum leaves this morning and offered him the liquid—not much, but enough to wet his throat—and some witchetty grubs, the dingo just turned away. I have never seen Pupa do that before—he has been with me every day since he was a pup and has slept curled up against me every night. In a rock hole high on the mountain, just behind the ridge, I found him, a skinny scrap sucking at the carcass of a bitch caught in a steel trap, and though that was long ago, animals are wiser and remember injustice better than do we humans.

The water hole over there, behind that huge boulder, is not a spring, but a clay-bottomed pool among the rocks into which the

spirits, coming from the lake far below, would tip any water left in the *piti* they had carried up the hill. It looks . . . yes, dry, dead leaves are piled on the cracked clay where water should be lapping. We won't bother to struggle down there and tire ourselves for nothing.

The line of the creek loops across the country—like a dead snake— from the mountain to the farthest edge of the sky. A line of trees grows from the dry creek bed and along the banks, but only a very few branches bear any leaves now. Some trees have shed their bark, too, and the trunks, dry and bare, look like a band of skeletons moving across the country. I can see the windmill from here, still upright and marking the halfway point between the mountain and the homestead; perhaps it still turns, trying to suck another drop of water from the ground—if there's any left to draw.

There's no smoke coming from the homestead. Tiwa must be out in the bush gathering *kaltu* seeds, and though so little of the grass has grown here for so many dry years, if there is only one stalk in the bush with one or two grains in it Tiwa will find them. She will grind the seeds into powder and bake *nyuma*, a loaf of damper, in the hot ashes of the campfire, for Tiwa knows that is a man's favorite tucker. If you should ask any of our fellows—any of the whole mob you can see in the sky at night—every single one would tell you that a man could wish for nothing better than the smell of hot *nyuma.* Life is good in this country just as long as the *kaltu* grows a good crop of the seed for making *nyuma.*

The wheel of the windmill is spinning still and the pump squeaks again and again, like a possum trapped in a burning log, but the end of the pipe and the troughs below are dry and coated with dust. Lying about—still waiting for water—are cattle, but only bones are left, poking through the dried and broken hides. It must have hurt the Boss to see his whole herd end that way. That man would go halfway across the country to catch a dingo that had been savaging his calves, and when he had destroyed it the poor animal would end up spiked on a stick or a broken tree so all might see the object of his revenge. There was no need for such display, however, for our spirits knew well that one of their number had suffered. Dingoes are not just animals to us but totem, and therefore sacred. Each dingo you see, or hear howling in the night, is a tribesman sent back to his tribal country to roam about until he happens upon one of his relatives, to whom he becomes guardian and companion.

Pupa still drags himself along behind me, but now even he must be convinced that there is nothing to fear. The homestead is deserted, and gone is the Boss who hated dingoes; who would shout, even when Pupa was a tumbling pup following me about: "Get rid of that murdering yellow devil."

I kept Pupa in a small shed, here under this big tree between the homestead and the creek, but now the place is bare, empty. It wasn't much of a shelter: just a couple of corrugated iron sheets leaning against the trunk of the tree to fend off the wind and the sun, but it was near to Tiwa, and she often came running down from the house with some tucker for me and Pupa. She brought us an old blanket once and we had a water bag, too; it had a hole in the canvas, near the top, but it held enough water to share between the two of us. Tiwa brought us a piece of bread now and then, made from the flour that the Boss kept in bags in his house, and though Pupa would eat that tucker he likes *nyuma* made from *kaltu* seeds much better. I sometimes think that the dingoes returned to our country just to harass the cattle and sheep, which eat everything that grows. When the beasts have swept through the country not a single blade of grass is left behind, and when the *kaltu* is destroyed, so is the tribesman's independence.

As soon as Pupa could trot he took on his responsibilities and chased calves, until one ran up from the creek and around the homestead. The Boss dashed out with his gun, held the pup in its sights, and was only distracted by Tiwa pleading and crying for the dog to be spared. The man glanced at the weeping girl before he fired, and his bullet hit the animal's leg. Pupa lived, but he was never again agile enough to chase calves.

The corrugated iron remains of the hut are still lying about on the ground, rusted and bent. There is an old petrol can by the tree and . . . yes, it's full of water, and underneath is a bundle of old clothes. These are the Boss's old trousers, I reckon, greasy and with only one button left; and his hat is here too. I've never worn a hat before, but it will be good to shield my head from the hot sun. Tiwa has thought of everything; she has even left us a loaf of bread, stuck there in the fork of the tree, and though it's as hard as a rock, when I splash it with water it will soon soften up and make good tucker for me and my old friend here. See how he wags his tail, now we are home.

Wawa, My Brother

The road had come to an end. I hadn't wanted it to, but there is a power greater than that of man or spirit which pushes us to go. Books may tell us why the life of humans is not made to last, like that of the rocks. I should have asked Wawa; he could have told me all about it, or some of his wise friends could, but it does not matter any more.

The whites are gathering quite a crowd—I never thought there would be so many of them to see me off. I have been given a whole church and a hard oak table to rest on. There is not much to be seen of me but a flag dropped over a mound-like shape. From underneath you can see the flickering of candles and hear the crackling sound of burning wax. There is a small gap under the cover, and the line of mourners can be seen flowing around like a silent river, all dressed in dark clothes and grim-faced. Sir Rock is dead! Every man and his dog knows by now.

Where does one go from here? The whites don't say much. Near me Wawa holds his book in the air: "He is your shepherd by choice, not by birth." The whites call him Bishop. Today he is dressed in his best clothes, and he's brought out his cross, books, and other sacred gear. He's gathered a whole bunch of young people to chant while the bell tolls . . . everything he would do for one of his fellow whites—even more, I reckon. "I brought this man out of darkness, my Lord. . . ."

Wawa has begun to talk. He is my brother not by birth or skin but because he was kind to blacks. Grief has struck him hard; his voice still shakes, but he will gather enough strength to see the ceremony through. He has stood next to me during the last two days and nights, seen the end of several candles, lighted new ones, and whispered gentle words to his spirit boss to be good to me.

". . . . and I have led him to you."

Some days ago when he dropped the flag over me he sighed—the sound of a wounded heart. Half of our lives were spent together—yes, it would be that long since he first came to Namanama, our tribal country. We cut a sapling in the bush and helped him stick the pole in the ground and place a cross on the top of it. Every tribesman came to give a hand; even Marngit, the medicine man, offered to help. My wives made a big fire and cooked yam in hot ashes; they even brought a dilly bag full of turtle eggs, but no salt. Why do whites always need to sprinkle a pinch of it over their food? Maybe to drive away *wardu*, bad spirits, who can sneak down the throat into the body and steal a man's soul. When you are a stranger in the country and your spirit boss is far off there will be a flock of sorcerers around. However, the salt did the trick—Marngit thought so. He is also *wawa,* my blood brother, and could not tell anything but the truth.

"Take him for good or bad, my Lord."

Does he know that I'm not flesh and bones now, but a mound of hardened dust? It scarcely bothers me; up in the bush at Namanama you can change into a boulder, tree, or cloud, but here . . . the whites would not like it nor would their spirit bosses. Last night Wawa walked around the oak table, tucking the loose ends of the flag under me, whispering some words that were not so much a chant as fear, I reckon. He must have seen me—I heard him mumbling: "Let's be quiet about it." Maybe no one else knows anything about it, and if it stays that way they could sneak me into the spirit world. Let's hope no one will peep under the flag or lean on me.

"He leaves behind a wound in our hearts." Wawa's voice trembles, then is drowned in the sound of bells. Why so much pain? We're going to meet again. Not here at Namanama, but in that spirit world he told me all about. I could give him a hand again to put up his cross and . . . no, I don't think either of my wives will be there to make a fire. I could help him cut saplings and make a hut. He will bring a hatchet. The whites are proud of their steel tool, which is much sharper than our stone *galdi.*

"He had faith in You and Progress." Wawa lifted his head so his voice would float high into the sky, the place of the white man's spirit world.

The bells boom and the whites chant. Such a crowd! But no black faces. Pity that Marngit, my tribal brother, is not here to see this. Perhaps not all are my friends, but there are more people here than I or any man at Namanama could count. He should not be angry with me, not any longer. When a man goes, you don't throw a spear after him. Wawa should have made sure my tribal brother was here, and a few other black faces to see all this and talk about it. Marngit—nothing would escape his eyes and ears, and when he went to the bush every soul in the tribe would know how heartbroken the white man was to see me go. Yesterday the Queen called here to light a candle, and her face seemed puffy—she looked as though she had been sobbing for days. She had known of me . . . perhaps long before I had ever heard of her. The whites too, like all our spirits, have *dal,* the magic power to see into the far distance and know all about your life before you meet them. She had her mind on me, all right: she sent Wawa a long way into the bush to bring me the hatchet. What a blade—it can fell a sapling with a single hit! No tribesman in the whole Reserve had one like that, and she asked for nothing in return. Yes, she also sent a box of matches for my wives. We never knew which one of the two the present was meant for.

Wawa lifted his book up to the sky: "He helped me build a temple to spread the word."

We made the church from logs and saplings. Marngit did not like it. At Namanama every tree is a black man, and to help Wawa put up his roof a whole patch of forest had to be cut down. At the back of the church we built a storeroom, all from rocks piled on one another. Wawa had some magic stuff, "gelignite" he called it. You need only a handful to blast the biggest boulder in the country. "The rocks are the souls of our ancestors," Marngit had cried. The medicine man said that some of the boulders in the country had been black fellows at Dreaming, the life long ago. Once, each of them had done something wrong, had harmed the country of the spirit world; Jambawal, Thunder Man, had come around with his *larpan,* magic spear, pinned the tribesman to the ground, and made him into rock.

"You gave us bread to hand to him."

Wawa had a small airplane, and whenever he came to the settlement he brought bags of sugar, boxes of tea, and tins of biscuits and locked the lot in the room built of stones. He kept tobacco there too, gave me and other men who came to church a packet each day. The women received a lump of barley sugar, my wives got a can of Coca-Cola, one to share. No one knew where it all came from. Wawa said it was Jesus, the white man's boss in the spirit world, who sent the goods and . . . yes, we always saw the airplane in the sky over the bush before it landed on the dusty strip near the church, and all of us waved. Whenever Wawa returned from his journey, the boxes full of goodies came with him. He asked for nothing to take away. Oh yes, he took a handful of chips from the blasted rock, placed them in a handkerchief, and tied the loose ends. Whether he took them for the spirit boss or the Queen, the chips were so little compared with all the goodies he brought to Namanama.

Wawa held both his arms in the air: "He gave us blood and breath. Each consignment of rocks from his native country meant new life to us."

Poor fellow Wawa, he had worked hard to see Namanama at its best. He learned how our country was made during the Dreaming. At the beginning of time, our ancestor Jambawal traveled across the black man's world carrying a dilly bag full of pebbles. He dropped one of them on the ground here and there, to become boulders. When he reached Namanama, the cord on his bag broke and the lot poured down. Namanama became rocky; no other country in the whole Reserve is so stony and hilly. Wawa wanted to make it into a better place, not for him but for us. He brought out a crowd of whites with machines—a whole flock of rattling beasts—and began to level the country, pounding every rock into dust. The tribal elders did not fancy the machines galloping about, and hated to see the columns of dust. Marngit was not happy either: "They'll chew up the whole country, as white ants do to a tree trunk."

The bell tolled.

Here I go, at last. A bunch of white men carry me out of the church on their shoulders. They move slowly so as not to jolt or upset me; perhaps they have not been told what I have shrunk into. Anyhow the whites are still bound to farewell me into the spirit world, even if I have changed into buffalo dung. Pity Marngit is not around to see this. Would he still be angry? He grew enraged at the whites blasting rock shelters and caves and feared there would not be a single place left in the country for man, spirit, or animal to shelter in during the Wet. The medicine man had gathered tribal elders and they chanted day and night, calling for Jambawal. They should not have worried. On part of the cleared country Wawa made a large compound enclosed by a tall wire fence, large enough for all the tribe to get inside. The place looked so secure even *wardu* could not have found a way in. Inside were piled Coca-Cola cans, boxes of biscuits, and bags of tea.

The men carrying me whispered something. Perhaps one of them had peeped under the flag and the news had spread about my new shape. What does that matter now? Wawa, the Bishop, knows what I am. The Queen knows too. So must Jesus, the boss of the spirit world, and . . . he will be waiting for me.

Pity no black face is around to farewell me—Wawa too would have been pleased to see some of the tribesmen around. He walks behind me with his eyes cast down. Marngit and the elders should not curse the poor fellow. He even made a shelter for our people, one for each black man—not a shelter like our caves or the homes the whites have but something in between. Each tribal soul was given a cement pipe with enough room to squeeze into and shelter from rain or wind. From above Jambawal can tear the sky apart and pour down torrents of rain, yet not a single drop will leak through.

The guns are booming; I'm not sure if the salvo is meant to farewell or welcome me, but whatever it is, black man never was so great. A fanfare of trumpets begins the march and the bells toll loudly enough to bring down the sky. If Jambawal is about, the noise will chase him away. No, I doubt whether he would have come so far. It is good that he stays at Namanama. If he were here, what would the whites do? You can't tame Thunder Man, not even if you give him scores of medals, offer boxes of tea, bags of sugar, bottles of Bacardi; even knighting him will not help.

The whole kingdom has stopped to see me off. People line the route, the crowd . . . I have never seen so many people before, all mourning. Some throw flowers toward me, others call a word or two of farewell. If each of those people shed only two tears, there would be a torrent in the street. No black faces yet. I wish they'd brought my wives, at least. Both of them would have loved the speech Wawa gave. I have never heard him talk for so long before. At Namanama the ceremony was much shorter. Whenever a black fellow passed away in the bush, Wawa would ask for one of the machines to come over the dusty land and dig a deep pit. Then he would gather around every soul from the compound and mumble: "Ashes to ashes, dust to dust." He always threw a handful of soil over the corpse and then would watch silently as the bulldozer pushed the rocks back into the trench.

My wives . . . yes, I can see them now. Not here but at Namanama, many skies away. No one else is in the compound and they . . . they look shrunken, with their skins covered by a layer of dust. Perhaps they have wallowed in the mud to keep the flies off or . . . yes, their skin may have begun to go white. They crawl about. Each has a concrete pipe and rolls it over the ground searching for shade, but there will be no shelter from the sun—the compound is as bare as your palm. Why struggle? Perhaps it does you good to hope.

I am placed on a trolley and pulled by a bulldozer. Pity the machine rattles, the noise drowns the fanfare of trumpets—even the bells can't be properly heard. Behind me walk a bunch of whites. Some of them I have met, others I vaguely know, and many I have never heard of. Yet all come to farewell me. The Queen has come too, hiding her face behind a dark veil, shielding the tears. The day

she knighted me was a happier occasion for both of us. She smiled then: "I will do my tongue a mischief pronouncing your native name—shall we just say Sir Rock?" She touched me with the tip of her sword, great day that it was. Let's hope the blacks and whites will remember it.

Right behind me walks Wawa, poor man, worn out and swaying. It looks as though he is treading over the rocky ground at Namanama. He has arranged everything. I know he will not let me down. That long speech he gave in the church helped a lot. Last night I was a bit cross with him—when you lie under a flag for days you begin to wonder if the earth has run out of room for you. I tried to remind him, maybe a bit harshly: "Wawa, aren't you taking me to your spirit world?"

"I have arranged a state funeral. You will be the first black man to have one."

"Do the spirits want me?"

"There are formalities—even the whites can't rush in at will." He sounded tired but not angry.

"You told me they would be waiting for me."

"We don't want to offend your former spirit bosses. They are already causing trouble. Can't you see your new shape?"

It is over now; I have to show Wawa I'm sorry for nagging last night. Perhaps when we see each other again in the spirit world I can make a fire for him to boil the billy. He doesn't take sugar in his tea, but a spoonful of tinned milk. Will they have kindling wood in the spirit world? The whites like to clear the bush and make the earth look like a skinned beast, but they should know that you always have to keep a tree here and there.

How far are they taking me? It's close to the end of the day and I am still on the road. That spirit world had better show up soon; the clouds are banked on the horizon, dark and leaden. That flag over me might give a bit of cover but it won't keep off the rain. A downpour could make a mess of me and . . . I don't want to change shape again.

The bulldozer sounds tired, puffs and coughs, but it is a tough beast made of steel. I'd better ask Wawa to hurry the machine; with a bit of luck we can beat the clouds. Look—he is gone! The others have left too—the Queen, the crowd, the lot. The bells have stopped, the trumpets and drums are silent. Only the bulldozer is still here, dragging me along a lonely country road toward a dark hole in the sky.

This could be the spirit world; it looks like the countryside with green paddocks and a tree showing here and there. A line of power poles stretches endlessly away. Yes, the spirits are all white and like to have the scene they know best around them. No scrub country around here to hunt a wallaby in, and I don't think there will be any sandy beaches with turtle eggs. Sheep and cows are grazing around. When I'm out looking for food I'd better not spear them; Wawa told me the beasts are *marain,* totem, to the white man, and never to be touched. I don't think I'll need any food now—a mound of dust doesn't eat—but with a bit of luck I could harden into a rock and live forever, just like the boulder at Namanama.

Lightning flashes and thunder rolls across the sky. Jambawal! The ancestor sounds moody, angry, roaring around the countryside. His *larpan* strikes the ground in front of me. A ball of milky light appears and moments later, instead of the bulldozer, there is a pile of twisted steel.

The storm has ripped the flag away. What a downpour! My shape! The mound is being washed away rapidly and down I go along the lonely country road. I wonder if Wawa knows of this—there is no one about now. Perhaps . . . yes, they must have made a deal with Jambawal—the mighty get together now and then when they have to send you off.

Cockatoo Man

Good has come after all—my ancestors, the spirits, have changed me into a cockatoo. What a bird! My feathers are full-grown, shiny-clean, and the pinions. . . . I'd better not stretch out my wings too far, there's not enough room here to display them properly. The walls are too close, moldy but strong. This place looks like a burrow, but it's made out of concrete with steel bars to keep you in. The light comes in to tell the time of day and the air flows in and out but a man is never likely to leave this place unless the spirits are about to fetch him out.

I won't stay close to the bars—Sergeant could be peeping in. The whites like to spy on everything; even if you have shrunk into an ant and have to crawl about for the rest of your life, they'll still think hard and long before letting you free.

The whites shouldn't worry; what is there to be angry about? Cockatoos can live for days on a handful of seeds. That should make Sergeant happy, the man . . . yes, he is around. I hear him stamping across a small yard and then his steps hurry down a short passage. He does it once a day—pushes a food bowl under the bars and hisses "Bloody boong! The rest of us have to earn our meal."

No, I don't think he's seen me. He never peers into the dark or stays long enough to hear my breathing. The man might see the empty cell tomorrow or the day after, but by then I'll be far away in the country, free. I'd better wait for a while before flying out. There's not much to be seen outside, only a corner of the yard and part of a high wall. A tall tree grows inside but it can't be seen from here; it throws a shade at about this time of day, with a bundle of leaves dancing for a while on the bare concrete, before that too slides from view, leaving the sun to bounce from the hard ground.

It's a good thing the tree is around. I'll head toward it, and when I crawl up the branches and glance over the wall, I'll be able to see the whole settlement again. Yirli, my wife, will still be down at the dry river bed, a good two voices away from here and a bit far to see her, but the smoke will give away the place where she camps on the sand under the tree. A few flaps will set me flying and then I'll glide down through the air—that will be all I have to do to reach her. No, she won't mind seeing me as a cockatoo; the bird is our totem and it would be bad only if the spirits had changed me into an owl or a crow.

A small flock of pigeons must have landed in the yard; I can hear their cooing—yes, there's one of the birds on the concrete at the corner searching the ground. I'll slip out through the bars and mingle with the flock; pigeons are a different size and color from me but we all fly, and when we're grouped together it's easier to notice any danger. The whites often like to set traps and you're never safe—whether you walk, crawl, or fly. Only the spirits are able to sneak in and out without fear.

If Sergeant sees me getting out like this, he'll eat his heart out. Though even if he were right here, the man would find it hard to work out what has really happened. He only believes what is written in his books or the words told by white Boss, the man they call Magistrate. Years ago when I tracked for Sergeant we saw a flock of cockatoos gathering around a water hole. The birds should not be disturbed at their drinking place; no man of our tribe would try to frighten them off. "They are all our people, some of them tribal elders—you don't chase them off," I tried to explain.

"How can you tell if a bird is a bloke or a gin?" Sergeant laughed.

The whites don't want to know a single thing about our world, but Sergeant should have been different. He has been here . . . came to our country not long after the first corrugated iron hut was built and saw the whole place grow into a settlement. The two of us have been together a lot to track our fellows, not only around here but deep into the bush, even to places three lingoes away. Once we

caught up with a fellow far off in the desert . . . yes, that was Mirna, my wife's brother. Poor man, he was tracked for days; I don't think he remembered when he had time to stop and gather tucker for his last meal.

"He'll never make it back to the settlement. Boss, what about a piece of biscuit for the poor bugger?" I asked.

"Why don't you gather some seeds; isn't he one of your cockatoo mates?"

One of the pigeons flaps its wings and flies up to a branch; the rest of the flock stays on the ground but each bird lifts its head up . . . no, they're not frightened of me, perhaps a shadow or some noise on the other side of the wall. I wonder what tucker one can gather from concrete. There are plenty of dry leaves floating around, but I doubt many seeds will be found. The tree over there is old and grown high—almost under the armpit of the clouds—but it does not seem happy any longer; a whole part has dried out. The dead wood, stripped of bark, looks like a long scar stretching from the lower fork to the bottom of the trunk. One of the low branches looms over the yard; it is quite thick but there is not a single leaf on it. I doubt whether a man could ever reach that branch from the ground—Sergeant must have had a hard time throwing a rope over it to let the noose hang down for a step or two. He never said anything about anyone being hanged here but . . . Yirli, my wife, she saw a man swaying on the end of a rope; it was dark and she couldn't see the face but it was one of us, who else could it have been?

One of the pigeons has found some food and struggles to pick it out from a crack in the concrete. Is it seed? Or perhaps Sergeant might now and then throw a handful of scraps into the yard. I've never seen him being nice to birds, but . . . the pigeons coo gently, hard to know whether it is a plea or a song—no man could be hard on them.

Now and then Sergeant used to chuck some food to me and Yirli. He let us inside here whenever the jail was empty, and even brought out a blanket for us to lie on and a flagon of . . . I'm not sure what kind of drink it was, very strong stuff, you didn't need much of that to send you to sleep. Whenever I had had enough of that plonk, I'd go to the end of the yard, down a short passage, and crawl into one of the cells behind the bars—the Sergeant liked me to do that. I could hear him in the dark, huffing and puffing for his life; when making love that man panted like a dingo trapped on hot sand.

I'd better get off the ground, cling to the rough bark of the tree and crawl up the trunk. I'll try not to flap my wings; the whites will be around for sure, and if they're in their hunting mood, they could bring me down from even the top branch. Yes, a lot of the bark has peeled off; the tree will have quite a struggle if all those scars are to be healed. Maybe the tree doesn't want to keep on growing. It has been around for a long time and already has seen too much. Down near the stump, Sergeant stuck a whole row of heavy bolts into the trunk so that he could chain our fellows whenever there were more of them in than they could fit inside the cells. I wonder what happened to them. They never stayed here for long, not even long enough to heal the scars they got from being hunted in the bush. Yirli thinks some of our fellows were given to Magistrate and he sneaked them out of the country to his big boss—"God," they call him—but Mirna, her brother, didn't go that way. His spirit must be around here—he comes now and then to have a chat with her in dreams.

That man, Magistrate, wears glasses. He lives right there, just behind that back wall. The man keeps a cockatoo, not like the one I have changed into, but much larger and black, with a small red patch hiding under his tail. When he's up on a perch, it looks as if he has been speared and the feathers stained with blood. Magistrate keeps him in the front of his house, chained to a veranda post. The bird reminds me of Wati, our tribal elder. He keeps his eyes half closed most of the time as though he has seen much of life, not only ours but those of my grandfathers and even the men before them. Whenever I walked along the street Wati used to whistle to me and one of his eyes would blink, telling me to come closer.

I should climb farther up the tree; a couple more branches and . . . I can see the house on the other side of the wall now but only the back. I don't think Wati will still be on the veranda; the chain must have long ago worn out or rusted and Magistrate—the man was gray and withered years ago. He used to snooze in a hammock stretched between two trees in his front garden, and a bottle with a cord around the neck hung on a sawed-off stump always within reach of his hand. Whatever was in that bottle made him snore so loud—it sounded like one of those saws the whites used to cut down the trees to build the first huts in the settlement. I was only *titi,* a boy, then, but once you hear the sound of dying bush, it stays with you forever.

Without bark, the smooth wood has hardened up like bone. I must cling to it and not slide down and made a noise. Long ago I used to sneak in from the front gate, pass the snoring man in the hammock, and tiptoe to the verandah. Black cockatoos eat wattle-tree seeds, the tucker they like best; I'd always bring a handful with me and scratch Wati behind his crest. The bird would stretch out his neck, lean his head on my chest, and whisper: "Go bush, you fool!" He did not like me hanging on to the white man and called often in my dreams to tell me that I should not track our fellows. He knew all about it—the name, tribe, and lingo of every man I helped Sergeant to bring in. "They'll get you in the end, you fool."

Once they grow old the whites go back to their country or to their boss, God—whichever way that works. Their house stays behind here to rust and rot. This one will not rot so easily—rocks last a long time. We quarried them from far across the river and dragged them over here, load after load; quite a job that was. The whites rounded up every black man, not only the cockatoo mob, but fellows from many lingoes away—everyone was here to blister his hands. If any fellow dared to run, Sergeant would follow quickly and track the poor soul to the far end of the country or to his last breath, whichever came first.

Not much will be left of the hammock; cords rot fast. No, the thing is still there, swaying slowly. Maybe the whites brought a new hammock when the old one wore out and . . . Wati! He is still here—I see him through an open window, in a cage now, but lucky that he has not been taken away with the old man to a far world or that God—wherever the whites have to go at the end. Someone else must have taken Wati over and . . . no, Magistrate is still about, moves around with the help of a stick and knocks with it against the cage: "Whistle for me 'God Save the Queen.' No food or water until I hear it."

Wati backs into a corner. The feathers on his back . . . many have been stripped and the bald skin looks red.

"I have to take you to a show. The people will clap and take pictures of you if you whistle the tune well."

Wati's head tilts away from the man's voice. Magistrate pokes the stick inside the cage and holds the cockatoo against the wire mesh while at the same time pulling out a handful of feathers.

The bird's crest fans out in anger: "Old white bastard."

I'd better not hang around here but go back to the trunk and climb up—the farther from here the safer it will be. A few more branches to go and I should be able to see the river. I wonder why Yirli has not made a fire. Perhaps she doesn't want to give away the place where she camps. You just dig a pit in the sand big enough to crawl in and hide; if you only come out at night to sniff around for food and your skin is black, the whites will hardly notice that you are around. I dug a burrow in the river bank after I left Sergeant, not big but enough room for me and Yirli to squeeze into. We covered the entrance with a big branch with dry leaves; it kept the sand from blowing in and hid our place. How did Sergeant find us? I wonder. No one of us saw him around, but the man must have sneaked in quite close, with a flagon in his hand, and spilled some of the stuff on the ground—strong booze, it lured me out of the burrow. Some of it was splashed here and there to drag me on and I tracked it until . . . yes, it led me right into that jail cell.

Look, there's going to be a good view from the top part of the tree, not only of the settlement but the whole of Ianala, our tribal country, and the land beyond, stretching to the far end of the sky. The walls down below now seem far away and the concrete yard . . . it looks like the bottom of a deep well. I wish I had met Wati much earlier and had not done so much tracking. There will still be some of our fellows around, not here but far away, right behind the mist that edges the sky—it will be too far for Sergeant and every white man to reach. Black Wati could fly there but only when he is let free.

A few pods have stuck in a fork of the branches. Yes, there are still some seeds in them; I'll stop for a while and pick at them. Sergeant has grown very mean with food lately. In the last few days he called he brought nothing but water; you don't live for long on that stuff, whatever you might be, human or bird. I should climb up farther; there might be more seeds around on the branches, and if not, I can fly off to. . . . No, there are no more trees to land on any longer. There used to be a whole bunch of huts scattered throughout the bush, but the settlement has gone. Instead, tall towers rise up, molded out of concrete, steel, and something else; they don't have the shape of a house but of a tall stack of boxes piled up to the sky. Why do the whites have to flock like that and make the place a big anthill? Maybe they're afraid that if they spread out through the country, our spirits might rise from the bush and take them on. They send Sergeant out to the bush to hound the black fellows, but he won't be able to do much if there are none of our fellows to track for him.

I hope Yirli is not angry with me. Though we never talked about her brother Mirna or any of our fellows, even if she felt angry the hard thoughts might have gone by now. As soon as I find her we'll head for the bush, a lingo or two away from here. The whites might not have got so far yet, and there should be plenty of trees there to bring flowers after each rain, and then, when the country grows dry for years, there are always some seed pods to be found.

Look, there's smoke down the river . . . no, it's not a fire but a machine puffing it up. It races through a dusty plain and looks like a mad beast. Something has happened to the river; the whites must have taken it away or channeled it under the ground, and all the trees have been crushed into dust. The ground looks flat and stripped like a shaven beast. Tomorrow or the day after, a flock of new buildings will spring up, each with a flagpole and a tall antenna piercing the smooth skin of the sky.

Far below, the steel gate of the jail squeaks. Sergeant has come in and brought . . . it's Yirli! There's not much left of her; she has shrunk down to the size of a wallaby with dusty skin and no fur to shield it. She crawls along slowly on her knees and elbows and struggles for breath with each step forward. It looks . . . she is just about to give up. Sergeant tries to hurry her. The man holds a limb of prickly pear and presses it against her back, but instead of moving, Yirli's body slides onto the concrete. I should screech, just to let her know that I'm around; she might not hear well now, but I could fly close, come down between the walls and hold on in the air with my wings and . . . no, I'll wait for a while. Sergeant is already dragging her across the yard and down into the short passage. It won't be long now before the man slams the gate and leaves. Then I can fly in, walk through the bars, and hang around until the white man calls in again, if he does. Lucky they never got around to chaining me up the way they did Wati, that old black fellow.

Babaru, the Family

Our Mother has left us. She has not died or run away but has changed into a crocodile. Maybe it is better that way—not that we will see much of her but it helps to know that she is not far off; should anything like that happen to any of us we will be around in the bush together again.

I hope Padre does not find out what has happened to Mother. He says that whenever any of us leaves we go to Heaven; the white man's boss called Jesus boils a huge billy in a campfire and the people, black and white, sit around and sip tea—you can put as many lumps of sugar in your cup as you like.

What should I say to the other children? There are two more of us—Anabrn and Purelko—and they are still asleep in the sandpit behind the fire, curled together like a couple of puppies. Mother called the pit *murlg,* the shelter, though it is nothing but a sheet of corrugated iron stuck sideways into the ground; it makes no cover from the rain but is a shield from the cold winds at night.

The sun has shot spear-high in the sky—the children will be up soon; they will nag me about Mother and ask for food. I had better see to the fire. A big log lies partly sunk in the ashes with a cluster of red coals buried beneath it—a few pokes with a stick and a chunk or two of wood will make it flare up again. I'm glad that Mother thought of it when she left; I was half awake and saw her waddling over the dusty ground. Her tail was swinging around the fire, slashing the ashes now and then; a log was clamped in her jaws, then dragged and pushed over the dying coals on top of the mound of ashes.

One of the children mumbles something; it is Purelko, my brother. He struggles to move his hand through the air to . . . tell me, perhaps, that he knows about Mother too. The boy, the youngest, is often awake at night and stares at the fire. When the flames go out he calls; sometimes he jerks his limbs to make me and Mother get up and do something about it. When we find food I have to feed him, the same as Mother did—hold a piece of yam in front of his mouth and wait for his lips to stretch open. With *njuga,* the mangrove crabs, you have to break off the tough pieces and chew them for him first. Padre says the boy will never get better; once a child is crippled like that he will be no different when he grows up.

Mother will be back, for sure, not now during the day, but at night. She will sneak in to check on the fire and see that we are all properly buried in the sand to keep warm. There is a big hole dug under the chain-wire fence, just over there at the far corner of the compound where the ground makes a small rise. Lucky the ground around is sandy and it is not hard to break out. She won't be far off; perhaps she's hiding in the mangroves farther down toward the bay.

Look, Padre is already up and has gone to open the gate. He only does it once a day for us to go out and look for bush tucker, but never so early. The gate squeaks—it sounds like a possum trapped in a hollow log. Once it leaves the compound, the track forks: one path goes up the river, passes a patch of thick forest, and leads to the scrub country stretching inland; the other branch follows the shore, passes the old jetty, and swings around the water. The outline of the bay looks like a badly thrown boomerang that fell short of coming back—as if it had hit the sea and made Warngi Cliff there across the entrance to the inlet.

Padre wears a white shirt and a dark wide-brimmed hat that has swallowed half his head. I saw him dressed like that long ago when Nati, Mother's father, left. Padre must have thought that the old man was on his way to Heaven and he gave him a good farewell, but Mother says our people go a different way.

"Should I come to sweep your hut?"

Mother did so every day. She made his fire and boiled the billy for tea. Once she even climbed up on the roof of the hut to prop up a

sapling with a cross on top of it and fasten the lot with a piece of wire.

"Don't worry about it."

"We can bring you some wood from the bush."

"You will have plenty on your hands looking after those two. You're about grown up now."

Padre pats me on the cheek and walks slowly to our shelter. A track of freshly disturbed sand stretches from the fire right to that hole under the fence, but the claw marks can't be clearly seen. Good that Mother dragged her long tail to sweep the dusty ground behind her.

"How is the little albino; growing up?"

Anabrn steps out from the pit and allows the man to pat her on the head. She has fair hair; where she has slept a seashell has left a deep mark on the pale skin of her neck. Why does he call her albino? Mother thinks it means "white," but . . . all three of us show a bit of it. Padre says that some children will turn completely black only when they grow up; perhaps that means when they become *bala,* initiated. It should be about time for me to go through that now. There is a place Mother told me about, a billabong, I think, far off in the bush where the bay plunges its foamy snoot into the land. The men from Dulbu tribe sit on the ground in the shade of paperbark trees and sound out their *bilma*, clapping sticks, and didjeridu loud enough to please every spirit in the country. The sound tells you that the time has come to go there and be made into a woman. I hope there is somebody there to tell me how to go about the ceremony when the day comes. Our Nati will be there with his *bilma* for sure. By now he must be *marngit,* medicine man; he will know about us coming to life.

"Here is some tea and sugar. You still have that billy, I hope." On the ground near the fire Padre leaves two half-full jars and then stares into the ashes for a while. Look, there are paw marks on the ground from Mother's webbed feet; they are the same as those of ducks and other water birds but much bigger.

Purelko is up and crawls around the fire. The boy tries to tell us something but can't make the words; he just mumbles a sound or two. Maybe he is asking for tucker—his face is stained with charcoal and a layer of sand is stuck to the wet skin around his mouth. Even though he is crippled, the boy should know that you don't feed on sand whatever the color of your skin—black or white.

"Raunga, see that the boy is fed."

Padre walks back to his hut without saying more. He might come out later in the day to look around and tell us what to do. I should go up the rise there and cover that hole beneath the fence; it might be better if Padre knows nothing about it. Even if he does guess what has happened to Mother, let's hide the way she has gone. The man might be angry because she has not departed the same way as the white people do and he could set a trap to catch her when she comes back to see us tonight. Our Nati told us that the whites like to hunt every living soul in the bush. I have never seen Padre kill an animal but once long ago I peeped into his hut, and there was a stack of crocodile hides inside—I doubt whether the beast can live after you have skinned it.

If Nati were here he could tell us a lot about crocodiles. The animal is *marain,* sacred, to him and to all of us. The old man hardly said anything to Padre, and when he was here he kept away from the hut—his fire was behind that dead tree right over there on the top of the rise. Look, it is still there; the wind has blown off the ashes, but two partly burned pieces of wood remain on the ground. Mother thought he had gone back to his place along the long arm of the land stretching from here into the sea and had walked over to Warngi Cliff where the *marngit* should be. You can see the hill far across the bay, showing up above the forest like a cap of dark cloud. He will be down there now sitting on the rocks, clapping his sticks and chanting to call the spirits from Bralgu far across the sea to come back and look after us and the animals—the whole country. When they come, the spirits will bring *dal,* magic power, to heal Purelko and everyone else who needs help. I wish Nati would hurry them up; without Mother I may not be able to feed the poor boy.

I should climb up on that dead tree and look out. I did it a season ago and went up to the top branches. The arm of land stretches far out into the sea and then curls around the bay and ends at Warngi Cliff—it looks like the tail of a huge crocodile swinging about to poke at a monstrous porpoise asleep on the sea.

Let's push some sand in and fill up the hole. If Mother comes back at night she will dig it out again. Crocodiles have strong claws; they can burrow into the ground like anteaters and often make hollows to lie and wallow in. Look, Nati has left his *bilma* behind; I have never heard him chanting without them, but even if he does, the spirits might not be pleased to hear the voice. The sticks—just plain pieces of wood—must mean a lot. Look, they are smooth and worn from being handled for so long. The pair have been around . . . the man before Nati, and the healers before him, must have chanted with those sticks.

Padre has come out of the hut again; I'll rush back to our fire and not let him come this way. The man has brought a bundle of rags and hands it to me: "Each one of you must make a 'lap-lap.' Girls should have a cover."

Mother wore a cover made of a burlap bag and it had a few holes where patches of dark skin showed through; she called it *maidja* and . . . a fire caught her cover once and burned a whole chunk out of it. She did not wear the bag around here but had to put it on whenever she went inside the hut.

Maybe a barge is coming today and Padre is in a hurry to clear out the hut and make room for new goodies. No boat has been here for many seasons; when it sailed in last . . . I doubt whether Anabrn or Purelko were born then. Yes, that is why Padre is dressed. I wonder how the man found out these fellows are on the way here. Perhaps Jesus came in his dreams last night and told him that goodies are on the way.

"You can have some blankets; there are a few inside."

When the boat came before, there was a tall pole behind the hut with a long piece of wire stretched to it—a magic string. Mother reckoned it went all the way up to the sky to let the white man talk to his boss. They called it "radio." Padre never had to chant and clap with sticks—he talked into the wire instead whenever he wanted a barge to be sent here.

"Where's our Mummy?" Anabrn looks down to the ground and her voice quivers.

"Raunga will tell you that."

"Has she gone to the river or the sea?" The child is shy—dashes behind me and covers her face with both hands.

Padre walks off and, passing through the gate, turns back: "If I'm not back by evening, go inside the hut."

Maybe he knows about Mother and thinks she will come tonight to snatch us all. Our Nati thinks the whites are tough on crocodiles, and Padre may not be so different from that lot. Pity, he was around here before I was born, and even before our mother was born. Only Nati remembers him coming to Dulbu country. The other old fellows would have known about it too, but all of them are long gone. They say the white man landed from the sea, washed up on a small sandy patch among the boulders on the other side of Warngi Cliff. He was stiff like a log, with no word of our lingo to tell us where he came from.

The water has slipped back from the shore, leaving behind a long stretch of mud and sand—the bay looks like a water tank with the tap left open. It will be noon or even later before the sea comes back and the first waves show up; by then I will have gathered a whole bag of *njuga,* enough for a much bigger *babaru* than the three of us.

Perhaps I should go up to the top end of the bay while the shore remains dry, and then come back to look for tucker later. The old man doesn't like to wait and the quicker I go the better it will be. If . . . let's leave Purelko under that whistling tree; without him to carry I can run.

"Rest here, boy, the sand is soft and shaded . . . Anabrn will look after you for a while."

"Can I gather some crabs?"

"Do, but . . . don't let him crawl close to the water."

Anabrn did not ask where I was going—perhaps she knew that I had *bilma* with me. The sticks are in the bottom of the dilly bag that hangs around my neck. Nati will be pleased to have them. In the bush there, far beyond the bay, the other old men will gather too; a whole flock of them will sit near the billabong to chant and . . . how can they sing without *bilma?* I've watched Nati chanting in camp many times. He claps the sticks one against the other a few times and then throws his voice high into the air so that it floats above the forest and across the bay to the land beyond. The *bilma* clap now and then to warn the spirits to be on the lookout for his call. A chant like that is magic, and when it is well sung it can not only heal humans but also bring back to life the dead trees and boulders scattered throughout Dulbu country.

Someone has just passed by here. Stretching along the shore toward the top of the bay there is a line of footprints in the wet sand: Padre—no one else around here wears shoes. Maybe he has gone for a walk. It will be quite a while before the tide comes in, and without the waves the barge will never be able to sail in. The boat has to come in right there, where those two rows of posts are stuck in the mud holding up a long platform made of saplings. There is hardly any water there now, but once the waves come back the sea will almost reach the top of the stilts. Padre calls it "jetty" and it has been there ever since I can remember. It must have been quite a job to drag all those trunks from the bush and sink them in the bay. All our fellows stuck to the job and struggled for a whole Dry to build that thing.

Mother didn't think that the jetty did any good, even though the barges called in a finger-count of time. They were loaded all right—our fellows had to drag bags and boxes of goodies ashore and then farther on up to the camp. Whenever the boat called, Padre's hut became like a hollow log packed up with honey. You only had to walk inside, look at the cross and whisper a few white man's words, then come out with a piece or two of barley sugar. I often got a handful of biscuits and learned to chant a little song, though I've never found out what the words meant. The women with small children each received a tin, not easy to open and the milk inside was too thick and hard to pour out—but it tasted nice. Mother often got a billycan full of flour; the powder had something . . . you could not tell if they were maggots or tiny weevils, but once the stuff was baked it tasted all right. Once she made *nadu,* damper, from . . . never knew whether it was dried milk or washing powder. Whatever the food came in, it always had shiny lettering on it to tell you how it should taste, but in the whole camp only Padre knew how to read.

Look, there is Padre, far away across the big bite of the bay; only his white shirt shows up, bobbing along the shore. He has gone a long way, almost to the patch of mangrove forest where the top part of the "tail" stretches out to bridge Warngi Cliff and the rest of the land. It's a tricky part of the country to go through—not so bad now, but once the tide is up the sea surges beyond the shore and moves inland through the mangroves to flood a whole chunk of the country. The water would almost cut off the whole of the cliff then if it were not for a long ridge of dunes that lies behind the mangrove forest shielding it from the open sea.

Yes, the *bilma* are in my bag all right. The sticks are our *ranga,* sacred, and when they are clapped, only old men and spirits can understand what they say. I hope Nati will not be angry with me—we all know that woman is not supposed to come to this part of the country except to be initiated. He may not be at the billabong; the spirits often go over the dunes to fish or look for oysters. If Nati is not there I will leave the sticks and . . . when I get back to the camp he might appear in my dream to tell me when I should go to the billabong again.

Should I tell Nati that the boat is about to come again? No, the old man might not like the news. The last time the barge was here it brought in a pile of timber, stacks of corrugated iron sheets, doors, windows, and rolls of wire mesh. Padre wanted to build a church—nothing like that hut but much bigger. The building was to sit on that rise in the compound, and the whisper went around that once it was up Padre would climb to the top to look right over the forest to the billabong to see what our spirits were up to. He put the wire fence around all right to make that compound but went no further. The church is still down in the bush near the jetty. You can't see much of it now; the piles of corrugated iron have been swallowed up by vines and scrub, and as for the stacks of timber—the ants have eaten the lot. The windows are still there, hiding behind a thick cover of leaves, and it is only now and then when *walu*, the sun, peeps in that the glass blinks back to say the stuff is still there.

There is not much sea here, only one arm of water that has moved in from the main body of the bay to separate the shore on this side from Warngi Cliff over there; it looks like the tongue of a panting animal. The cliff looms above, tall—almost halfway to the clouds. The rocks facing the bay go straight up like a wall. The whole hill has the shape of a whale, and it was indeed once a *warngi,* sea monster. Our Nati says that at the Dreaming, the time when the spirits were about to make Dulbu country, a huge sea beast rushed toward the land to snatch them. One of our ancestors, Crocodile Man, rushed out from the billabong over there in the bush and dived into the bay. He moved about under the water for a while, and when he showed up again his jaws were wide open and he snapped at the monster, taking out a whole chunk before *warngi* could even see him properly.

The cliff side facing that small stretch of land. . . . Look—Padre is stuggling up the craggy slopes and . . . he will not have far to go before he reaches the top of the wall. Quick, I'd better leave the shore and walk through the bush; I don't want him to see me. The billabong should not be far off now, tucked somewhere in the bush between here and the edge of the mangrove marsh.

I wonder what Padre is doing here. Maybe he wants to have a good look from the cliff to see how far out to sea the barge is. The boat might be passing Dulbu country and taking goodies to some other place; he will have to shout out or wave to make the white fellows call in. Before, there was a tall pole on the rise at our camp, and every time the barge was due to call, a flag flapped on the top. It helped, but the pole has long gone and . . . Padre might take off his shirt now and wave with it from the cliff to bring his fellows this way. Yes, that is what he is doing, I can see him between the branches; his shirt must be unbuttoned—it flaps about in the wind. I wonder how long he is going to be there. The tide hasn't turned yet, but it shouldn't be long before the waves come rolling across the shore to the mangrove marsh. It will be hard to get back from the cliff then.

I'll wander through the bush and look for the billabong; it can't be far off and . . . I hope it shows up soon—I'm getting thirsty. Padre might feel that way too. There won't be much to drink among the rocks there. His fellow whites might have forgotten about him and may never come. Mother says he spoke angry words to his boss. It happened not long after the barge was here last time and something went wrong with our people. A few children died first and then a whole mob of us, young and old, got sick.

"It's a plague—could wipe us all out!" Padre used to yell into the magic wire—you could hear his voice right across the camp. "Send us bloody doctors and medicine—come quickly, for Heaven's sake." His voice was heard for days. It seemed as though he would choke himself with the loud calls, but instead he grew angry and. . . . The radio was thrown out of a window and broke into pieces as it hit the ground.

"Bloody Doctors" never came. Our Nati was right when he told us that the boat would not call again because there was nothing for them to take back from our country. A few bundles of crocodile skins were sent off but that was only a small crumb against all the loads of goodies that had been brought in—so little to please Padre's boss.

I have to kneel to get some water, maybe lie on the billabong bank and lean forward for a good drink. It is quite a big pool, well tucked into the bush. Huge paperbark trees have grown sky-tall, not so much to make shade but to hide the place from outside view. The ground over there near a huge boulder looks well cleared and bare—even the rock surface seems to be smooth, perhaps touched by humans and spirits alike.

Let's step about slowly; the men could be resting and elders do not like to be disturbed. They might be behind bushes, hiding in the shade, or . . . yes, they should be resting on the bottom of the billabong as all of our spirits do. I wonder if Nati will be there or . . . no, he is likely to be farther down at the top of Warngi Cliff. Look, there is a track going that way; the path swings around the mangrove marsh heading to the sandy ridge behind, and then a long neck of land heads toward the cliff. The old man must often come down here from the hill, chant and dance with the spirits, and then head back to Warngi—from there you can keep an eye on the whole Dulbu country.

I'd better be off. I'll just leave the *bilma* stick on top of the boulder and come in some other time when they want me. Look, something has just moved in the pool. On the surface two flower buds float; no, they are a pair of green eyes and . . . yes, the snout is over there—crocodiles often surface from underneath the lily pads to get a breath of air, and they don't show much of themselves if they want to rest in peace.

The sea is back, with the waves racing one another and rolling toward the shore. It will not be long now before the water slides over the small embankment and pours in to flood the mangrove forest behind. Padre should be down from the cliff by now if he is ever to come back. Maybe he has gone to the other side of the hill. Mother told us there are pieces of an airplane washed up on the shore there and stuck among the rocks. The metal does not rot quickly and could not be eaten by ants. The wrecked pieces have been there since "War," Mother thinks. However long ago that was, it is much further back than she remembers. When the airplane plunged into the sea it had aboard a whole bunch of white men. Maybe some of them made it to the shore farther up the coast but no one ever heard of them; we wouldn't have known about Padre either if Nati had not found him.

The sun is already hanging down from the sky; it will not be long now before it plunges into the sea. I'd better hurry back—Anabrn and Purelko will be angry with me for leaving them so long. They could already be calling for me, but children have weak voices and . . . they grow feebler when you are worn out with hunger. It would need to be like the roar of a didjeridu, not just a voice to match the howl of the sea, to reach this part of the bay.

Look, a white cloth lies washed up, the waves are still splashing against it: Padre's shirt—no, only half of it. His hat has come in too, sitting there on the water as though looking for the best spot to come ashore. Perhaps . . . Padre must have gone to see Nati and our other fellows. Good that they took him with them; he has been in our country ever since that day when Nati found him on the shore. The man must be too angry to go to his boss. Better this way; we may not see much of him, but now and then he will show up in our dreams.

I'll pick up the shirt and hat and take them down to the jetty and leave them on a log there. If the barge comes this way again the whites can have their clothes back.

Warand, the Dingo

I have never heard what a trap looks like. It is set for animals, perhaps people as well, and whoever it snaps shut on does not live to tell how it was. It is a man-made beast, not so big: two steel jaws each with a row of teeth—I can feel them with my fingertips. They are ghastly; it will be a struggle to break away from their grip.

It must hurt, that caught leg; Warand does not show much of it now. The animal has given up struggling to break free and licks his front limb at the knee where the steel teeth must have gone through the skin. Yes, he licks my hand as well; perhaps he thinks I am caught in the trap too. What can I do, I wonder. My *mauwulan,* walking stick, has been broken into pieces; I tried to force it inside the trap and push the jaws apart but wood is weak against steel. Maybe there is something better to be found than a piece of wood. My *duwei,* my late husband, used stone: "With tough rock you can wreck the trap with one blow, it rips the guts out of it," he told me. A pity there are no rocks here; maybe there are some farther up in the bush but it is hard to find anything when you are blind.

I won't go far away; with no one to lead me now, I could wander off into the bush and never find my way back. Before, whenever I felt lost, I only had to whistle—Warand always came on my call. Even if the dingo was a voice away from me, he would rush back and lead me to the right track. Duwei says the dingoes are our own people reborn—they come back to life as animals, hoping they might do better that way. They have thick fur to keep them warm at night, and when they are out looking for tucker, they will catch up with a wallaby much quicker than any of our fellows with their spears, but . . . yes, whatever luck the dingoes had did not last; the country has lately gone hard on all of us. Whether you are a human or an animal, the whites are out to trap you just the same.

Warand yaps; perhaps as I am moving away the animal is warning me not to wander far off and . . . I might never find my way back. Dingoes not only stick to you for life but follow your mind as well. We had a whole pack of them long ago when we lived near the Homestead, about a couple of camps away down the plain. The animals used to clear out at dawn so they wouldn't be seen by the stockmen, but even if they went to the far end of the country, they always returned at evening to lie curled up against us when the night grew cold. They slept with their ears pricked up, not so much out of fear—the whites do not hunt during the night, but my husband talked in his sleep and the animals were keen not to miss a single word. The dingoes would have been right: when one talks in his dreams he is not only telling what is on his mind but brings us a message from our spirits.

Warand still yaps, though the call sounds a bit faint now. I should go back and give the poor fellow a cuddle . . . no, I'd better look for a branch or two with some leaves and hurry to make a bit of shade over him. The sun is getting very hot and the sandy ground will soon be . . . it will feel like treading over hot ashes. On a day like this it will not take long for the heat to finish you off. What will I do if he goes? We stick to each other as two do when there is no one else in the whole country left to cling to.

I'll wave the branch over Warand to cool him a bit. . . . He sighs, throwing out a whole load of pain, then licks my leg. Duwei told me that dingoes are like humans: when hurt, they suffer just the same as we do. Once a dingo bitch did not turn up in camp at the end of the day but instead showed up the next afternoon. She came on three legs, followed by a swarm of flies, and crawled up to lie beside us. Duwei gave her some water and went to look for tucker, but she had no strength to open her mouth; only her eyes tracked us about trying to tell us somethng. . . . Yes, the wound was a bit much and she gave up. No, I don't think Warand will quit like that; he is a tough hunter, used to wandering through the country every day. He has dodged more traps than there are trees around and has always made it back to camp with a catch—a small goanna in his mouth if nothing else.

Poor Warand leans his head against my leg and sighs; I can feel his heart beating fast as though fighting for breath. I wonder how he let himself be caught today—he knows every single bush around here. There is a water hole down at the gully, about a voice away from here, and he leads me there and back every day. Before, we had to sneak in only at dusk or dawn for a quick drink and to fill our billycan while the stockmen were not around and then follow the track back up the gully. There is a rock shelter high up at the foot of the hills, the shadiest spot in the whole country for animals and people alike. No, the whites hardly ever came that way; they don't like to struggle over the craggy slopes. Perhaps they were afraid that our spirits might still be hiding behind the cliffs and would push the rocks down on them. From the cave we used to hear the stockmen on their horses galloping across the plain beyond the water hole mustering their herds or . . . yes, the whining sound of the truck struggling through the bush. Whatever it was—animal or machine—Duwei always kept his eyes on the trail of dust the stockmen left behind, and if it was headed this way he and the dingoes would dash from the shelter and sneak out farther into the hills.

The end of the trap is chained and bolted to a tree stump—no hope of taking that off and letting Warand drag the steel jaws about. I had better go and look for some water before the dingo pants away. The sun is like a boiling billy resting on top of our heads. The water hole should not be far off—I can hear a flock of *lindaridj,* galahs, busily chatting at the drinking place. The birds are never tired of making a noise, and the sound will show me the right way to move. I should find a new *mauwulan*—a small branch will do if nothing better—just to have something in front of me so I can feel where to step. I wish this were only a dream, long and hard—the same as those Duwei often had when he struggled in his sleep and the dingoes' ears were up like spears to catch every word. He never told me what the dreams were all about and I don't think the dingoes learned the secrets either. It was about us I reckon; this water hole is the only one for many camps around. It used to hold enough water for a much bigger *babaru* than the two of us and all those birds and animals that called in from the far bush, even many voices away, until the cows were brought here. The white man's beasts drank most of it and we always feared that next time we came around looking for water, there might be nothing left but a muddy patch.

The dingo howls; maybe he is trying to let me know how far away I have gone, or perhaps he wants me to hurry back with a drink. On a day like this you could not hold out for long; Duwei did hold out for a finger-count of days however, but he did not have the whole of his body in the sun. The stockmen chained him to a large boulder, there beyond the Homestead, and there was a shady patch under it for shelter, but only big enough for him to squeeze his head and chest underneath. I wonder why they chained him; they say he stole a horse, but it is not one of our animals and you never go close to a beast of that size; it gallops through the country like a willy-willy, and even if a whole tribe of our fellows were around, the spears would not be fast enough to catch up with it. Yes, Duwei might have tried to scare the beast off and not let it hang around the water hole, but . . . no, I don't think they got him because of that animal. When the whites left the Homestead not long ago, a whole pack of horses was left behind to do good to no one. I could not see them, but now and then I can hear a thundering in the bush and I can't help fearing that the stockmen are back, but as the sound of hooves fades away like a wild wind you soon come to know—no man is around, only the beasts left behind and gone astray.

There is plenty of water in the hole; it is not hard to dip in the billycan now. Before, with the cows around, the hole was half full at its best and I always had to struggle through thick mud to scoop it up and then plunge my hand into the billycan to feel how much silt was in it too. No, I will not lose myself here, I know every bit of this ground and move about touching it like my own skin, and . . . there should be a few stones around the edge of the water. I remember them before, covered with mud and often splashed with dung, but they should be well dry now, and one of them will not be hard to carry back, if I can only find it. No, I will not wander off from this place; the *lindaridj* are around, screeching all the time—a whole flock of them and much noisier than ever before. Perhaps the birds are trying to tell me how good it must be to have the water hole to ourselves again. A wild horse or a donkey might come now and then, but not those herds of cows to muddy the place and make the water's edge slide down to the bottom.

The dingo howls again; it sounds more like a cry now than a call, worn out and faint. Perhaps I should hurry back, but the stone is a bit heavy to carry. I will get it there moving a few steps at a time; the bigger the stone, the better blow it will give to the trap. It will be just as Duwei did it when he was around. I went to see him every day when he was chained down to that boulder and brought him water

and tucker. I was still able then to plunge my digging stick in the ground and gather some roots. I even often got a handful of witchetty grubs from around the wattletree stumps. He liked that tucker better than anything gathered from the bush.

There is no howl to be heard now. Warand must have given up, or perhaps he is resting for a while and will call out again. I know the part around here well, and I should be getting closer; he might have seen me coming already and maybe he is wagging his tail now. If I can't manage to wreck that trap I will have to rub the chain against the stone and break it. I tried to free Duwei that way too, though the links were much heavier, but we did it in turn, each of us having a go and then resting while the other rubbed the steel against the sharp edge of the rock. We made quite a groove, halfway through the link, but . . . I had to go and bring a billy of water, leaving him behind. He seemed not so keen to struggle when he was left alone. Perhaps he feared that even if he did break free, it would not be long before he would be caught again and brought back to the boulder and . . . yes, the more you struggle, the harder they press on you. He came to see me the following night in my sleep: "I'm off to Dreaming; our fellows have come and freed me."

The spirits whisked Duwei away; once they see that you are stuck hard they do not sit and watch you suffer forever.

The stump is here all right and the pieces of chain that were bound to that trap. The steel is terribly hot, lying on the sand; I have almost taken the skin off my fingers by touching it. How poor Warand must feel; perhaps . . . no, only the leg is left, with flies buzzing around it and blood splashed over the steel jaws. He has bitten off his limb and wandered off to the bush. I had better sound out a few calls to tell him I am back, give him some water and get a leafy branch to keep those flies off. Later we can go back down the gully and camp there—it is all our country again, and although it might not bring much good now to either of us, it will ease our wounds to know the land is ours.

I'll sound out more calls, and if he is not back by the end of the day, Warand will turn up in my dreams for sure.

Balandja, the Cockatoos

The water rests still; it sits on the valley like an immense carcass rolled down the hill during the last Wet and trapped there, with nowhere to go. Something must have happened to the river; it does not flow any farther. Down at the bottom of the valley there should be two large cliffs on opposite banks making a gap. The rock might have slid down and blocked the way, turning the whole area above into a lake, but it has never happened before. The river has always flowed through, not only in my lifetime but long before—during *lalai,* the time of the tribal spirits.

Perhaps I am not back in Gidja, my tribal country, but am wandering somewhere else where not even in my dreams have I been before. I might have gone . . . not mad, but a bit strange, the way many old women do when they grow older. It happens to animals too; even the dogs become blunt before they pass away.

There is a hill across the water floating in distant haze; it should not be far away, but when you don't see well things around have a strange shape. The whites have given me a pair of glasses, but they are useless if you try to see your country through them; perhaps they help you to knit or read if you know how. The distant hills look like a cloud gathered on the horizon with their craggy outline and . . . yes, it is Gidja country all right; I have often worried that I would never make my way back and my spirit would be left to wander in that white man's world with no *djojmenu,* place of its own, to go to.

That hill across the water—it is all one rock, huge like a mountain; we call it Anguban, the Cloud. It should not be far from here, less than the reach of a cockatoo cry—pity there is no way to cross the murky water; it will take me days to walk all the way down the gap and around the lake.

The water of the lake has gone down a good way lately, leaving a strip of bare mud with the dry surface already looking like a shattered slate and serpenting all the way from the fringe of the lake to the edge of the ridge looming over it. To go on you would have to beat a track no one has ever trodden on before, no man, animal, or . . . even a spirit would hate to wander this way. I had better watch my step—the ground is soft beneath the crusty surface and my foot often plunges deep into the muck. I wonder if there is better ground to walk on. Up on the ridge there is a plateau that leads all the way down to the gap, but the edge of the escarpment is very steep; I climbed up years ago as a child to look down the valley but I could not make it now.

A flock of birds has sprung from the plateau, flown above the rocks, and dived down into the valley. They are *balandja,* white cockatoos; I have not seen them in a flock for ages, only in cages. The birds swing around and flutter their wings in the air above me. They screech now and then, and the call echoes against the cliffs and floats above the lake that once used to be a valley. The cockatoos are the first to notice anyone coming into Gidja country, and now the news is about the people who will come out to meet me. There must be some of them around; the tribe was a large mob.

Something must have frightened the *balandja;* all at once they screech and struggle to rise high up in the air. They are not scared of me, I hope; it's been years, almost a lifetime, since I used to catch them. I was only a young girl then, and the birds should know that, they have a better memory than humans; when they are young, you can teach them to talk. Not long after the whites moved into the valley, at the canteen down at the surveyor's camp, they used to give three bottles of Coca-Cola for a young cockatoo chick, and often you ended up with a handful of barley sugar as well. The man behind the counter used to pat me on the cheek whenever I brought in a bird. We wondered why the whites were mad on *balandja;* perhaps they wanted to teach the chicks to talk and then let them go back in the bush to follow the Gidja people. Perhaps the whites wanted to know the secret—how our *maba,* the old man, chanted the rain-making ceremony and danced to bring water from the sky; everyone in the tribe thought he could do that.

The birds have come down to perch on the top of a tree, where it sticks out above the water and shows the bony color of wood but no leaves or bark. They watch me struggle along the water's edge and then . . . they are up in the air again, flapping with their wings to get high up and then heading across the water toward Anguban, the cloud hill. The birds must know that I am heading over there and want to show me the way. The cockatoos have blue deep eyes and seldom blink; they have seen a lot and know more than humans. Most of them have come from our mob—when people get old like me and not good to anyone around they make their way over there to Anguban to rest for good. There is a *bandja,* a big burial cave, under the hill and as soon as one of us goes in for good, a cockatoo flaps out from the crags and glides down to the valley to join the flock.

The sun is heading down to the hills and a good part of the day is gone. I should start looking for a place to rest; moving here is like walking along the edge of the billabong when the long days of Dry suck most of the water out. There used to be a large billabong just over there, stretching alongside the escarpment—quite a swamp, nearly a half-day long and a bird cry wide. When you looked down on it from the ridge above it did not seem a billabong at all but a clear patch on the plane of the green valley. It looked as though a crocodile had come out of the river, crawled through the bushes, and stretched itself to sunbathe along the foot of the cliffs.

We used to come to the billabong often to gather the water lilies and search for tortoises. And the pelican came always at the beginning of the Dry, not long after the *wulun*, the paperbark trees, had lost their blossoms and set the nectar floating over the valley, riding on the inland wind. We camped right there under . . . yes, at the base of those huge trunks. The charcoal from the fire will still be there; it never dies—it is like the rocks, but the mud sits on top of it now. The *wulun* trees . . . all seem to be there, with the bottoms of the trunks in and the rest out of the water. Poor fellow trees—no leaves or bark, just bare branches.

The *balandja* are back. They flap around and beat their wings in the air, and then the whole flock gathers on a dead tree. They are like children—they shove each other around and grab the best place to perch, they nag and argue, the branch under them snaps off and splashes down into the water. They are back up in the air again, screeching and arguing; they swing around me, the nagging lot. Perhaps the *balandja* are trying to tell me something—what has happened to Gidja country and where the people have gone; the birds would be the ones to know it all.

The edge of the water comes right up to the wall of the cliff and the strip of dry mud ends there. I shall have to climb the rocks and go along the higher part of the ridge slope; it is not hard, I still know how—you hold onto the rocks with both legs and hands and force yourself forward.

The view is much better from above; every tree in the valley can be seen now, the whole forest floating on the shadowy dark water. Some have lost their upright line and halfway down lean their bony branches on the trunk next to them; from here they look *jadara ameri-gamari,* like propped goannas. A long sheet of red plastic, carried by the gale from somewhere across the water, is wrapped around the branches of a tree; the loose ends flutter in the wind and lash against the gum's dry skeleton. We used to come all the way here to look for young cockatoos. A man, Snow they called him, with hair the color of straw, drove me around the valley in his Land Rover. Wherever we went we carried a hatchet; cockatoos nest in hollow tree trunks, and often the upper part of the tree had to be chopped off so that I could plunge my arm inside the trunk and reach the nest. The chicks always come in twos; I don't know why—that is the way of the *balandja.*

The worn-out sun perches on Anguban for a while, then sneaks behind the hill to rest for the night. Flanked by the water the hill looks strange and smaller, as though it has been trimmed by the whites. The old men of our tribe say that long ago, before the birds, trees, or those rocks came to life, there was no rain for years. Whenever a cloud appeared on the horizon, Kakadja, one of the evil spirits, tossed a lasso made of hair at the cloud and dragged it away over the valley before a drop of water ever came down. One of our ancestors, Wondjin they call him, waited on those cliffs; he saw the cloud being taken away and threw his spear toward the sky. It was a good hit. The cord snapped, and the cloud stopped and then plummeted down to the ground; it still lies there, in the shape of that craggy hill. When the cloud fell to the ground, its water burst out and rushed down toward the sea, leaving behind a huge valley as it passed through Gidja country.

I wish I could make fire; then if there were any Gidja people still around, the light would be seen. We were shown as children how to spin a stick of dry wood between the palms and force it hard against a stump resting on the ground. It does not take long to make smoke if you know how. I should have thought of it earlier, looked around for the right piece of wood and. . . . Too late now: Anguban has almost sunk in the dark; only its rigid head shows against the red sky. They say the hill is hollow, with nothing inside but *bandja;* only the tribal elders were allowed to go in, but at the end, when death is near, everyone is taken there to rest.

The *balandja* are up with the beginning of the day. There are more in the flock now, perching on the branches of the dead tree. Some must have sneaked across the water from Anguban at dawn. It looks as though all the Gidja people have been turned into cockatoos—the birds are looking at the ridge toward me screeching madly. I wonder what they are carrying on about—perhaps complaining that the valley is sunk under the water. Cockatoos are not pelicans; they are after seeds, berries, and all that tucker, not fish or frogs.

I had better hurry along the slopes down to the gap and swing around to the other side of the valley; it is a long camp's journey to Anguban, if not more. The screeching of birds still bounces against the cliffs. I have never seen such a flock before, and so loud; perhaps all those *balandja* chicks that I snatched from their nests are back with their mob. The chicks were so small—they had no feathers at all, only a tiny growth on top of their heads which showed the coming of the crest.

I took them to the hut that Snow built for me from corrugated sheets and branches near the surveyors' camp. Every day he brought food from the canteen for both of us; there were plenty of biscuits—boxes of them—but *balandja* don't eat sweets and only like bread crusts. First I would take a small piece, chew it in my mouth, and then bring my head close to the chick; the little one would plunge its beak into my lips and grasp the food on the tip of my tongue. The birds thought I was their mother; at night they suffered from the cold and would totter around looking for me, crawling under my skirt to feel the warmth of my skin. I named each one of them—Hembularu, Olun, Laj, Omba, Chiri, Aru, Umudu, Shil, Tjarung . . . and often I whispered the names into the dark.

I should not have given them away to the whites; the Gidja people curse me for it. Maba says the *balandja* are our relatives and *lalai*—totem, the white man calls it. Many of those chicks I gave away found their way back to the bush again. You can teach cockatoos white men's words and even make them eat sweet food, but in the end they will fly back to their flock the way we all do.

The gap is not so far away now—just over there where the ridge has extended one of its arms deep into the valley, and it is almost the same on the opposite bank of the river. It looks as though the mountains have come down to hug each other and are locked in the valley. Look, I have lost my glasses. Perhaps I left them there among the bushes at the escarpment where I slept last night and . . . anyway I can see even better without their help. They gave me the glasses years ago in town; perhaps over there you don't see well because nothing is happy and bright to look at. Here, in Gidja, I know every single tree and rock; there is the spirit of one of our ancestors hiding inside each one and you know them by sound, not by sight only.

The gap looks wider now, maybe because of the high embankment of water from the lake leaning on it from above, or maybe the whites have done something nasty to it. The Gidja elders say that at Dreaming, the Beginning the whites call it, that nasty spirit, Kakadja, sneaked in from the plain at the lower part of the river and saw the tribal people by the billabong with a good catch of fish wrapped up in lily leaves and cooked in the hot ash of the campfire. Kakadja was always hungry and mad for fish—he rolled the hills from both flanks of the valley and blocked the river to drown the Gidja people so he could be the only one to feast on fish in the future. One of our ancestors, Willy-Willy Man, rushed from the spirit world to help; he

galloped down the valley, uprooting the trees and tossing the rocks in his anger, and with him rolled a mountain of dust sky-high that crashed through the embankment, leaving a huge gap behind to let the river flow through again.

The *balandja* cannot be seen any longer, but their screeching can still be heard from behind the rocks down at the water's edge. Maybe there are not enough berries and seeds for the poor souls; they cannot live on rocks and water, and the dead trees are not much help either. Their screeching sounds faint—it is like hearing the cries of children. Once Snow drove me far up the valley, past the billabong, and we wandered into a camp tucked in the far end of the river forest. All the fires had been dead for days. Only young children could be seen: some had already reached silence with a swarm of flies buzzing around their stiff bodies; others still had some life left in them to call out, but the sound was weak and faint like a whisper. The dogs roamed around the camp sniffing for food. I wondered what had happened to the grownups and . . . yes, Snow knew it—the whole tribe had been rounded up and loaded on trucks to clear the valley. The Gidja mob were resettled in some strange camp many water holes away. If you were a man it would take you a whole lifetime to make your way back.

I should have pleaded with the whites to take me from the surveyors' camp to the bush again with some food for the children, but no one had time for that—everyone was in a hurry to block the river gap before the start of the Wet. Look here, where they poured in a whole hill of concrete between those two cliffs; now you can walk on top of it from one side of the valley to the other. It is so high that if you roll a rock it rattles down the steep surface of the concrete for quite a while until it plunges into a pool, all that is left of the old river bed.

If Willy-Willy calls in again I wonder whether he will be able to knock down the dam wall and free the valley. The concrete is rock-tough and the whites have built in a lot of heavy steel and put in their sweat as well . . . yet nothing on earth could stop that mighty ancestor; he could gallop from end to end of the country and flatten the lot. Maybe he does not know the tribe is gone and the men are not around here any more to chant and call for him, or . . . even if he knows, there are lots of troubles for black fellows everywhere and it is a bit hard for him to catch up with the lot.

Anguban hill is not so far now; I will reach it before sunset if the heat of the day does not knock me down to the ground. I wonder what one does when one walks inside *bandja;* should I chant to call in the spirits or just sit, not nag or annoy them but wait to be noticed? I should have asked the old people—they knew how one should behave when going up to the cave. It was long ago when I was around here last; however, even though I thought then that this day would come, the elders were not keen on talking to me. They were right—I should not have gone on snatching the *balandja* chicks; once the birds had been taught to speak they said a lot. Cockatoos are very chatty; the whites learned from them all about the Gidja people, the Kakadja spirit, and the way he had blocked the gap to flood the valley. Once they knew about that, the whites did the same; they also took away all the tribal men, leaving no one around to clap the sticks together and chant, calling for Willy-Willy to come with help.

The water sits around Anguban and part of the lake separates it from the shore—you have to be a bird or a fish to reach the cave now. I should have known that. The hill rests on the valley with the plain around it. It looks as though a good half of the hill has been sliced off, leaving behind the sharp edge of the quarried rocks. I can see a dark patch on the reddish surface, half submerged in the murky water of the lake. It's *bandja,* or whatever is left of it. The block of *balandja* fly from the other side of the lake and swing around the hill; they flap in the air for a while and seem to be looking for a spot to perch, but they suddenly change their minds and head back, carrying the screeches in their beaks.

There is nothing to do but sit and wait. Perhaps I should chant with two sticks of wood in my hands, knocking them together to accompany my voice. Willy-Willy might hear that, and if he is not so busy fighting the whites elsewhere he will gallop in from the far plain to raze to the ground the concrete wall at the gap and free the valley again.

Dugaruru

It will be nice to be in Nakara, my tribal country, stretch out on dry sand by the campfire, and have an armful of straw or soft paperbark on which to put *yudu,* the child, when it comes. It would be nice to have an old woman who could tell me what mothers need to know, but if there isn't one, then the flickering flames or the spirits wandering about will tell me what to do: "You don't go that way any longer," the *balandas,* the whites, say.

The bed looks funny, and it sways a bit as though it is about to slip away from under you. I have never slept on anything like this before. I think the proper way to rest is to stretch out on the middle of it—that's the way the nurse placed me, and then she tucked the loose end of the blanket under the mattress and went quickly out. The woman did not say why they shifted me here—not much of a room, rather like a box with four walls and a door. There is a square of glass on a small shelf—*balandas* call it "TV." I would not say it is a window, yet you can see through it: people, trees, even the skies show now and then, or whatever the whites want you to look at.

The place I was in yesterday—a much bigger room halfway down a corridor—was packed with beds and had so many *balandas* around that the place looked like an anthill. I did not mind being among them; though the faces and the lingo are different it still makes you happy to know that there is someone a step or two away. They keep a large picture there of Boma, the Ripper, a whole wall of his smiling face. *Balandas* call him Dr. Tinto and . . . I wonder why they have to keep him here? Perhaps to greet the children and tell them what a beautiful place the world is to come into.

Why did the nurse have to shift me out, I wonder? She wasn't angry: "You brought us a headache here; c'mon love, get on the trolley."

The door is not locked but shut so tight, not even a breath of air will go through. Perhaps this is how all the whites are born, but it will be no good for us. My mother's brother, Wawa, says that before a black child can be born its *djuwi,* spirit, has to come from the sacred water hole and get inside your *walg,* the womb. Everyone at Nakara has come to life that way.

The nurse is back again, walking slowly as though stepping over a snake's nest: "I couldn't grasp how that stone got inside. It's quite a size, shows on X-ray—the doctors are gathering to see what to do. They've seen nothing like that before."

A tiny box hangs from her neck and makes pipping noises as she looms over the bed. The woman swings the gadget over my belly and the pipping noise grows louder; it sounds like a whole mob of chicks left without food ever since they were hatched. I've heard that noise before, not between the walls here but at Nakara, far away in the bush.

"Even Dr. Tinto is coming to the meeting—not that he knows much about babies but he knows all the world needs to learn about rocks."

Why does she have to carry that pipping gadget around her neck? In the bush that fellow Boma, the first white man I ever saw, had one like that but much bigger, the size of a billy though shaped like a box. He called it "Geiger." The box must be sacred to whites, I reckon—the man never parted with it.

The nurse pricks the tip of my finger and takes out a drop of blood: "Keep your eyes on the telly—Dr. Tinto will be on with 'An Address to Mankind' today."

The white man came to our country when my mother was still *wirgul,* a young girl. Wawa said he appeared with the passing of the Wet, slid in on the last rainbow from the sky, and hung around in our tribal country through the Dry. None of our fellows knew what the tapping noise of the Geiger was all about.

"Have you ever been to see a doctor before?" The woman still hangs around.

Wawa thought that in his dark box Boma carried the souls of his dead relatives—the same way as our old men do in the *badi,* the dilly bags you often see hanging from their necks. The spirits kept tapping from the inside, nagging at the white man to hurry through the bush and find a water hole for them; once on the bottom each one of them would find a *dugaruru,* a sacred stone, to sit on and wait for the time to be reborn. Our *djuwi* are not in a hurry, they can wait through many Wets and Drys—longer than any of us can remember. Maybe some of them would like to come to life sooner, but there are not many black women around to choose for mothers.

"Some tribal medicine man must have fiddled with you. The spookies can mess you up all right."

She should not think like that. Our old men were good, made no trouble for Boma—they gave him *wirgul* to make his fire and go around the bush to gather tucker. The man ate yams, well-cooked ducks, and yabbies. Mother even made him *nadu,* damper, from crushed cycad-palm nuts, though the tucker is sacred—you only feed it to black fellows during *nara,* the big ceremony, to give them strength to chant better and please the spirits.

The nurse is about to leave: "Keep your eyes on the telly—Dr. Tinto should be on soon. He won the Governor George Arthur plaque for his design of a human habitat, you know. It's all about your people, love."

Why do the whites have to worry about *yudu?* It's between you and the spirits whether it comes or not and when. They say even man has nothing to do with it. Black or white, he can sleep with you for a whole Dry and wear himself out making love, yet nothing much will come out of it. Mother thinks, however, that the man helps a bit. He opens you up, you both steam and smell—the breeze carries it through the bush and into *marain,* the sacred waterhole, to wake a spirit and . . . . When making love you look nice and happy—what better woman can one choose to come to life again as a mother?

How do the white children come about? None of that mob knows much about *dugaruru*—the *balandas'* spirits live in the sky and . . . no, they will not be about in the same way as ours. I should have asked my mother about that; perhaps she could have learned about it from Boma. The white man taught her many words; she even learned to read "Bacardi," "Gin," "Brandy," and roll tobacco quicker than the white fellows do. Pity she left while I was young. When I was left behind I should have gone to my father's mob, but there was none to go to, so Wawa took me to become one of his children. The tribal elders say it is our law to go that way—not at Nankara but in every tribal country all the way across the Reserve.

My belly itches. It shows up from under the blanket—huge like a boulder and . . . yes, hard and stiff. Perhaps I should get up and walk about a bit the way the women do in camp. That will make me feel well. Every one of us has to go through this, I reckon; if only Mother had been around long enough to tell me what it would be like. Perhaps she would have stayed with us in the bush if she had been allowed; our fellows say that once you begin to hang on to the white man's ways you anger the spirits and they chase you out from Nakara country. But . . . we will meet at our *marain* for sure, when the time comes for me to part too. The place is our *babaru,* family, and no one can push you out from there.

No, I should not walk out of the room, but let's just open the door a bit and look through. The nurse is over there—sits behind her desk and looks . . . yes, she's going through my *badi.* Maybe the woman is after my "wish." Each mother-to-be can ask for the child she wants: if she puts a tiny spear in her bag, a boy will come; a small digging stick will bring a girl. I never got around to making one—whatever happens to come will be mine and black.

The nurse takes out my bone knife and looks at it for a while. It has long gone blunt but you never throw away a tool, however worn, until something better comes your way. The woman now stares at the *dudji,* the firesticks. I don't think she knows what they are for. If you have never in your life had to spin the sticks to make a campfire, how can you tell?

Down the corridor they are pushing a trolley. . . . Look, Mother is on it! Her face has dried out and looks like a chunk of wood with the bark long gone. She must have seen me—she lifts her hand to call or tell me something, but no words come out and the hand stiffens in the air. Behind her rolls another trolley, and another—a whole line of Nakara women ride on them. They wear no clothes or covers and their skin, worn by the winds, shows patches of peeling crust. There are so many of them, young and old—they look like a flock of flying foxes seen at dusk when drifting toward the red sea of sunset. Now and then a hand or two rises up, perhaps to say something, but no words come. Even if they voiced them, the call would not be heard. The place around is flooded with cries, not any of ours but of young, newly born whites. There seems to be a nest somewhere near, with a huge pile of eggs, and the lot has hatched at once and is calling to be cared for.

My legs have had about enough. Let's go back, stretch out on the bed and . . . look, a man is on TV pushing a trolley with my mother on it. Her hand is still up in the air and he pushes it down hard.

"Dear fellow humans. . . . "

It is Boma. He looks tired though, and no longer wears shorts and a dusty shirt. His hair has turned gray, and it seems as though a huge seashell has been placed on top of his head. Slowly he picks up a small oval stone from Mother's body and lifts it up.

"An Aboriginal ritual emblem—each tribal member has one like this kept in the local water hole for his or her spirits to go to."

If Wawa were around he would spear him for this. Long ago when Boma was in Nakara country, he was told to keep well away from *marain* and the ceremonial ground nearby. Only the old men were allowed to go there, chant and clap their *bilma*, the sticks, to please the spirits resting on the bottom of the pool. Should anything happen to that place, Nakara people would be finished.

"The stones are high-grade uranium. A much smaller prototype of this has been mysteriously detected in the reproductive organs of tribal women."

They say *dugaruru* is hidden inside the *walg* in each of us, so that when the spirits come in they feel at home. Without the stone, none of us would ever come to life. It has been like that since Dreaming, the time when the first black people were brought to life. One man, then, called Bomaboma, tried to rape a young girl, cousin to him. Inside her she had a stone, just as every woman of the old time did, and that stopped him from making love. The man grew angry—grabbed his spear and ripped up her belly. Did him no good, though; when he died, his spirit could not find its way to Bralgu and

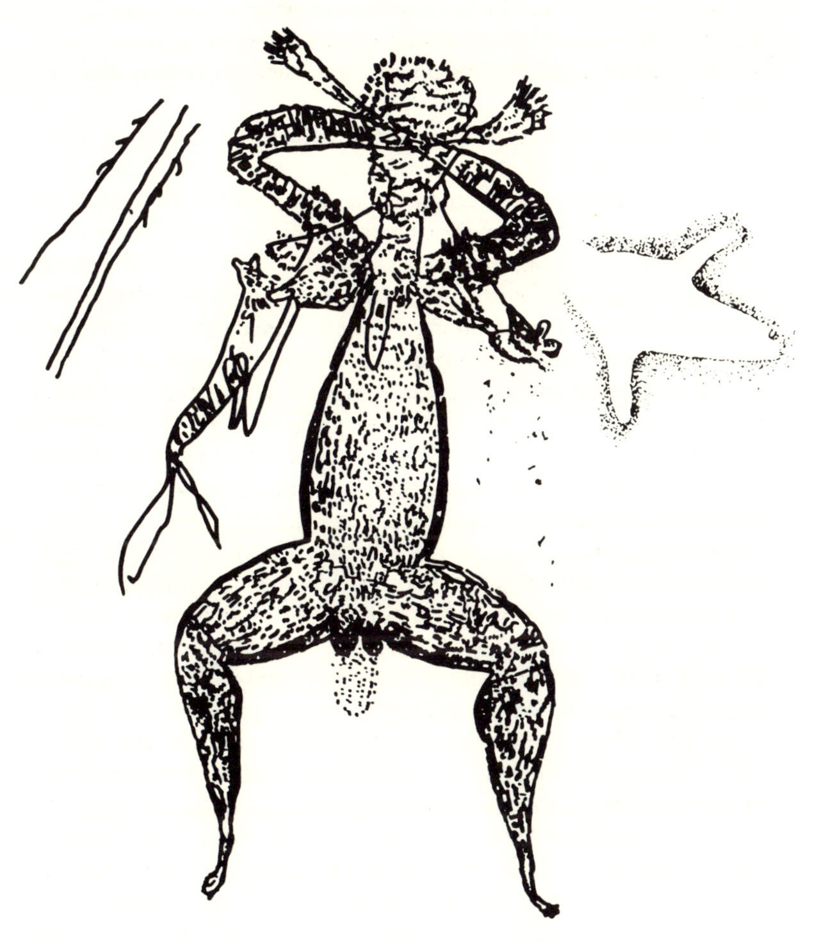

stayed in the country instead, to scare the women around. He often shows up like a willy-willy running through the bush, uprooting the trees and tearing the bushes.

I have not seen *dugaruru,* but some of the old women remember the stone. It was around when *nara* had to be held before the Wet so that Nakara would spring to life again. The stones were brought out for the women to pound the nuts on and then make *nadu* for our dancing men.

"We recorded a magic chant, the key for subjecting Aboriginals to this tragic plight."

On the screen Wawa is seen now blowing his didjeridu; it must be during *nara.* His chest is painted with yellow and red ochre to show the emblem—on skin, *dugaruru* looks like early sun struggling through the morning mist toward the open sky. Behind Wawa our chanting fellows keep stamping on the ground, raising a cloud of dust that hangs in the air around the palm fronds before drifting slowly across the land. The scene must have happened, but not now—the men have been long gone. There have been many Wets since, but without them calling for life to come to the country again.

"We mounted a manhunt to catch this villain; we will even go to his spirit world to have him brought to trial."

When he was in our country, Boma cleared a patch of bush, knocking down the trees and burning the scrub to make the camp. The whites do it that way; they are like the emus, afraid to rest in the forest, but fond of shearing off the country so they can see for many spears around. In the middle of the camp stood a large banyan tree planted during *wongar,* the beginning of the world, when our ancestor Djangawul made Nakara country. The tree has grown ever since— there are enough to shelter a whole *babaru* during the Wet. From branches the roots hang down and plunge themselves into the ground, supporting the trunk—no storms or angry spirits could ever uproot it. . . . Yes, Boma brought some nasty stuff, "gelignite" he called it, and packed some of it under the hanging roots. The banyan flew into the air, scattering branches and chunks of wood all over the bush. Part of the trunk was left behind, with the bark thrown partly off and left hanging down, like the feathers of a speared bird.

"We have been called upon to emancipate those people."

After he set camp Boma brought *warngi,* a flying monster with a gray belly and flapping pinions. It flew, just as spirits or birds do, but at night it always came down to a clearing behind the banyan stumps and shared the camp with the rest of us. Whenever it rose up or had to come down, *warngi,* "copter" Boma called it . . . yes, it left behind a cloud of dust and sent pieces of torn bark and wood chips flying from the stumps.

Wawa and the other elders called into camp to ask that *warngi* not fly in the country around *marain.* The monster could easily chase off the spirits and throw dust and dead leaves to mess up the pool. Without the spirits to come to life the whole country would turn into dust.

"We began to mop up the country. Every lethal stone like this has to be removed. . . . "

The monstrous bird hatched a whole flock, not of its own kind but crawling metal beasts, *dabalan,* "caterpillars" Mother called them. Whatever they were—monsters or machines—the flocks spread through the country sweeping away the trees, scrub, and rocks. Behind them hung a cloud of dust and a long track of crushed, bare land.

The *dabalan* gathered around *marain,* danced around it, and began to tear the ground apart. Whether they were fighting for a share of the water from the pool or wallowing in the dust no one could tell. Wawa and the other men went there to chase the metal beasts away but . . . they never came back. Mother says the men threw their spears but since they were of no help, the fellows went to Bralgu to call our ancestors.

"With the rocks taken away, the quarry will be filled with water and turned into an imense lake—miles of it to accommodate every Aboriginal spirit." The man placed *dugaruru* on one side of a small scale and then held Mother, withered and shrunken—no bigger than a pebble—to put her on the scale too. Her size came down further, fell into the shape of a bead and then into a speck of sand.

A picture of an empty honeycomb appeared on the screen with Boma's voice heard from behind:

"This is a model of a spiritual hatchery—it will be made of concrete and plastic and placed on the bottom of the lake. We will provide the sonar sound of the didjeridu and keep a constant temperature. Like this, the tribe can live for thousands of years—no scraps of food needed and no complaints."

They have placed me on the trolley now and are wheeling it along a corridor, not one I have been down before, but a passage molded in concrete stretching farther than your eyes or mind can reach. The nurse walks beside me for a while holding my hand; she presses into my palm a piece of barley sugar.

"Hold this, love; it'll sweeten up your life a bit."

My belly seems . . . it is flat now and rough; the whole body feels as though I am not touching it but moving my hand over the bark of a tree. The nurse is still around. She holds a large photo in front of me—it's that honeycomb picture again; "Look, what a fine calm place; all your flocks will be there." She leans over to bring her mouth to my ear. "The Authority has started extradition procedures, I heard on the wireless. Wawa, that awful old man, will be brought to trial."

The trolley is out of the corridor now and is being wheeled over a field of thick dust. It must be Nakara country—ahead of me stretches a long column. . . . I can see Mother on her trolley no bigger than a speck of sand, and the others are here too, the whole tribal mob, all on trolleys. My belly feels . . . gone! Not only it but the whole body—bones and flesh have shrunk into a flat stone. Yet it feels warm, as though the blood still runs inside.

Far away across the country of dust lies a huge lake—the head of the column has reached the shore already and plunges slowly into the water; it will not be long now before we are down to the bottom to sink into our *walg*. Yes, I have shrunk again. Only a speck of sand remains now, but it is still warm, telling of the soul inside.

Bungawa, My Master

At Murngin, my tribal country, the dingoes don't bark; they wander around, silently sniffing for food. Here I'd better not raise my voice; the town is an anthill crowded with whites, and you are one against the lot.

Do the whites know I'm different from other dogs? Bungawa, my master, cannot see the color of my hair and the shape of my snout. He always walks a step behind me, and as long as I guide him well, nothing else seems to matter. Today he has not said much, not even where I should lead him. Perhaps he has sensed that it will not be long before we part. Later on, in the afternoon, Jambawal, our tribal ancestor, will come to me. The whites do not dare say much, they even fear to talk of him.

"Where are we off to, my girl?"

Bungawa should know. The blind can feel and sense just as well as animals do. The seashore is still two good voices away and can't be seen from here, but you can tell. Behind us is the town—the sound of snarling beasts wallowing in the mist. In front lies the open sky.

"Of course, we have to 'see' the bulk carriers today." How could Bungawa have forgotten it—every second day I lead him through the park stretching between the town and the bay. There is a well-made path to follow, but even if there hadn't been one we would have made a track—we've been that way so many times. The path ends at a cliff overlooking the harbor, with the sea stretching many skies away. Bungawa sees nothing; he likes to rest on a bench and listen to the sound of bulk carriers coming in and out of the ore terminals.

"We could do with a bit of a breeze; hope the shore is not far away."

The days we don't come down here I take Bungawa to the Stock Exchange. It's a much shorter trip and I have a long rest, stretched on the floor of the trading hall. The place smells of tobacco and has a noisy feel about it, as though the whole world has slid into an abyss, and the whites are grasping to drag it back. What does Bungawa find interesting there, I wonder? He cannot see the titles and figures written on the blackboards, although he stares at them just the same. A few of his mates whisper to him what's going on, but I wouldn't fall for their words.

A harness holds me back: "Hold on for a while, girl. This sun is pitiless."

You don't move away from the shade when the sun is hot, unless you're being chased. Every black man and animal in the bush knows that. You keep under cover until the shadows grow long and the air mellow. Bungawa would know that; he has lived in Murngin for a good stretch of his life and has seen the bush—perhaps more of it than his eyes could handle before they wore out, though his eyes weren't much good to start with. He used to wear a pair of glasses—I didn't think he wore them to see through but to shield his face from the branches and tough spear grass when he rushed through the bush searching for rocks.

It's certainly a hot day; I will pant my life away. Good thing that we stopped to rest in the shade; breathing this air is like leaning over a boiling billy. There is going to be quite a storm later on—a cyclone, I reckon. Jambawal, the Thunder Man, brings it with him when he gets angry, and this time he has had to come a long way to fetch me. Maybe he'll be worn out from the long journey, and carry only a downpour, without rage and wind. No, the spirits aren't easily tired—you can go to the end of the white man's world, be changed into a fly or an ant, but you are always one of the tribal mob, and they will have to come sooner or later and take you back again.

"You get tired easily, old girl. Old age is catching up with you."

What will Bungawa do after I go? Get himself a younger dog, perhaps an Alsatian? No, they are a moody breed, and would snap at his friends at the Stock Exchange. The men are tough at that place—I've had my tail stepped on so often there that a big lump has grown on it, and however hard I try it doesn't wag any more. I said nothing. The whites don't like to hear any voice but their own, and what good would it do to show anger anyway? It only pushes you out of life a little quicker. That place, the Exchange, wears me out quicker than the hot sun. Perhaps it is because I can't follow the trading words and figures and staring at the walls makes you sleepy. And whenever I close my eyes to snooze, one of Bungawa's mates likes to tread hard on the end of my tail. I learned long ago to curl it around my legs, but that doesn't keep trouble away. Yesterday that same white man brought his cigar butt against my whiskers, burned two of them, and took off a piece of my skin with the glowing end. The whites around whispered for a while, then sniggered—they were planning to tuck a butt under my tail. It's a good thing I'll not be going back to that lot again, it'll save trouble for both me and Bungawa.

"C'mon, old girl, the sea can't be far away now." He swings the harness to make me hurry.

Pity we didn't start earlier, when the shadows were longer. When we were at Murngin, Bungawa used to get up at dawn, hurry me up to see that the billy boiled quickly for the morning tea, and then he would rush off into the bush to search for rocks. Why was he so keen on them? You don't eat rocks and nothing grows on them but moss and lichen. In our tribal country he used to chip off a piece of boulder and stare at the sample to see if it would bring him luck. Even at night when he was asleep in the tent he would mumble some words and pound me as though I too had turned into a boulder.

A broken branch lies across the path; I should walk around it and go easy. If he stumbles against the limb, Bungawa might fall over. He never asked about our child when I was *galei,* his woman. The boy had blue eyes—my mother called him Boss. She took care of him, even breast-fed the little feller, the same as she would her own child. I didn't see much of the boy—I had to go on through the bush following Bungawa while he looked for rocks—and we never talked about Boss. When you are given to a man to make his fire and keep him warm at night, you only speak when you are spoken to.

"The harbor sounds busy." Bungawa sat on the bench facing the bay.

Down at the water, two large ships had berthed beside the platforms of the ore terminal, and the machines hurried to unload the rocks from the metal belly of the bulk carriers. Farther out to sea three more ships appeared, outlined against the cloudy sky as they waited to be relieved of their cargo. The machines will need to be quick; the clouds are storm-laden and once they get here . . . I don't think Jambawal will notice what he overturns or smashes against the cliff.

"Here, rest under the bench, old girl; I'll buy you a new harness tomorrow." He speaks loudly so that his voice will not be drowned out by the noise from the rattling rocks at the terminal.

Will he be angry with me for leaving? When we grow old we have to go to our own people. The white world is too different from the black one—the spirits cannot make their home there. Bungawa must know that. When he's angry he doesn't say much, but he hisses through his nose. Years ago, when I had Boss, he was moody the whole Dry. We went across Murngin looking for rocks and making new camps, but he seldom spoke. The tribal elders should have told him that when a girl grows up to become *bala*, initiated, she turns into a mother. It doesn't matter what color skin or eyes the child has, it stays in the tribal bush and the campfire is its home. Whatever happens to the country, trees, rocks, and bushes, he will be a part of it. Perhaps it is better that way—if he had followed his father what would have become of Boss? The tribal children don't read the figures or names at the Exchange, and to sit here on the cliff watching the unloading of ore is no fun if your soul is black.

Jambawal rolled across the sky, rushing the clouds toward the shore. Here he comes, the mighty ancestor; I always feared I might have gone too far for him to find me. The tribal elders say Jambawal will travel to the end of the world to reclaim a black soul. Anyhow, I doubt whether it was hard for him to find me—he had only to follow one of those ships across the sea. The rocks at the terminal come from Marngit country. I have not yet learned why they are brought here; no one eats the rocks—perhaps the whites need them to throw at each other.

Lightning splits the dark mountain of cloud. Bungawa can't see it, but he must have heard the thunder, shaking both sky and earth.

"A good rain won't do any harm."

Bungawa doesn't seem afraid; he has seen Jambawal angry before, at Murngin. He says he lost his eyes blasting a boulder with "gelignite," but he had blown up the rocks ever since coming to the tribal country and never hurt himself before. I think the ancestor got tired of watching the white man splitting boulders and thought of a way to chase him from our country. Lightning was meant to frighten him off, but it was too strong and burned his eyes as well.

The sky split again, and the storm hit the bay. A wall of water rose over the ships and the terminal, swallowing the lot in one gulp. A wave leaped toward the sky, lashed the shore, and smashed against the cliff. Here was Jambawal to take me at last. I had to close my eyes and let myself be carried; it shouldn't take long . . . less time than a dream, and when I wake up I will be in the black man's spirit world. Every Murngin soul will be there—Boss too. Yes, our spirits don't mind if someone has blue eyes and freckled skin. If Murngin is your mother country, the spirit world is yours as well. The whites can take you many skies away and no matter what shape they change you to, Jambawal will be around to help you in the end.

The water has slid back from the cliff. My harness is caught against the bench and holds me back. Why didn't Jambawal free me? Perhaps—yes, far down in the sea a piece of torn shirt is caught on the rocks. You don't wear clothes in the spirit world any more than you blast boulders. Bungawa, my master, will be lonely there, among a whole crowd of blacks. Maybe . . . yes, that would be why Jambawal took him there.

Yudu, the Children

As they are born, children wail piteously as though their very souls are about to be torn from them, but no one has yet been able to tell me why. The whites have words to explain everything, if one could only believe them, and the tribal elders . . . they speak the truth but I dare not ask them.

Let's hope that this time it all goes quickly and that the screams will not be heard for long. The settlement cannot be far away now—maybe only two camps distant. Mount Djangau will show itself first, rising in the far distance like a cloud, but so clear that even if a traveler wandered blindfolded, he could not miss it. From here to the end of the sky, whichever way you look across the country, there is no hill like Mount Djangau.

It should not be such a difficult journey—just across the Galpu and Reyun countries—but with such a heavy belly it is like dragging a boulder, and for the sake of the little *yudu* I cannot hurry. Though unborn, a child can have moods just like any grown person, and this one gives me such kicks from inside, meaning no harm of course, but strong enough to remind me that when you are on the way to becoming a mother you had better not gallop about.

The sun is perched on the blunt edge of the forest; I had better stop and make camp, for there is a rock shelter hidden behind the pandanus groves, hardly half a voice away from the bush track. It is a good place to rest even now, but during the Wet it is especially so for it is always dry. It might look lonely and deserted now, but in the time of my mother and long before that—since the Dreaming, when the spirits moved about shaping the country and forming the rocks—the shelter was home for many *babaru,* families from both the Reyun and Galpu people. On my way to the settlement last time I camped here, and a season or two earlier as well—the rock gives shelter from the hot sun during the day, and at night feels warm, like a mother's breast. I will make a fire again tonight, not just because it feels good to watch the light of the flame dancing on the surface of the rocks and flickering among the branches of the trees, but because it makes sure that you are not alone in the bush. Animals, spirits, even white men wandering abroad will know that the fire marks this place as my home. A pair of *dudji,* firesticks . . . yes, they are here in my *badi,* dilly bag, and with them is the little spear, less than a handspan long, that I have made to tell the spirits that the child I want should be a boy. Last time I made a tiny *badi,* no bigger than a pandanus nut, and, just as I had expected, the girl Eanibugei was born. The name I gave her was that of the turtle I dreamed about when I first felt the child inside me, but I doubt that the whites call her that; not only will their tongues stumble over the word, but their teachings will aim to lead the girl away from her beginnings—away from the earth and the sky and the spirits from which she sprang.

I will gather some wood on the way to the shelter, and a handful of dry grass to catch onto the first spark I make with my spinning *dudji;* then, when the smoke is curling up, some twigs and dead leaves will be needed to coax the fire to spread to the bigger chunks of wood. Not all of us do it that way, mind you; Midinari, my *duwei,* uses soft bark instead of grass. He was journeying with me—not on the last trip but the time before, much earlier—and I remember that he as not happy to camp here at the rock. A wallaby was hiding under the shelter; our approach scared it off, and the animal went leaping and dodging down a scrubby gully. The wallaby is *marain* to Midinari—his totem—so he has never raised a spear against one and would fight anyone who dared to do so in Galpu, his clan country. But I . . . well, I yelled after the animal just as a hunter would do, and though I meant no harm, the cry upset him. When people become old, they grow particularly careful not to offend the spirits, perhaps because they do not know how much time might be left for the sin to be forgotten.

I had better look around for some bush tucker before darkness sets in. Behind the rock stretches a pandanus valley, and a voice or two farther down is a long-dry billabong. I might find some berries in the bush—even a handful would do me—but for some years now this country has yielded us little. The pandanus seldom bears any nuts and the animals have fled; it is as if the whole country is numb with misery at the white man's invasion. If there is nothing else to be found, I might have to look for grubs—there are plenty of dead trees around, their trunks hung with shreds of torn bark. What a sharp kick from inside my womb!—a few more like that will rip my belly apart. "C'mon now, my boy, calm down. Don't lose your temper with me." I must sit down. That anthill will do. The child should come soon—in no more than a few days I reckon. Aah, how he kicks! I can feel it on my palm held against my belly. The child must know I am on my way to the settlement, for even if there were no other way for him to sense it, the spirits would tell. I wonder how the white children come into being when none of that mob believes in the spirits. That's what they say—but maybe that hospital nurse is really the white man's spirit. She always wears white clothes and she says she is the same as *marngit,* our medicine man, but I doubt that—not because she is a woman, for the Djungau sisters were female and they helped their brother make the whole country. . . . No . . . she smiles too much, and even pats me on the shoulder. To be fair, though, she's kind. Whenever I have called at the hospital she has never let me leave without a load of goodies—whole bundles of bright colored clothes, with shiny buttons and zips; always a blanket, if not two; and food. Yes, boxes of biscuits, barley sugar, and some tobacco to take to my *duwei,* to keep the old fellow happy too. She even sent an ax for him once.

There is a hole as deep as a well right in the middle of the path here. It's lucky I did not step right in, for it must have been dug a season or two ago and is quite hidden with small twigs and dead leaves. A wallaby has fallen in, and only its bones and those of a joey are left now. Whoever set the trap never came back to gather his catch, so it was probably a white man; they so easily forget such things, if they have found something else to fuss about. A pump squats at the far end of the billabong, sucking water from the depths and pushing it through a pipe all the way to the settlement. The whites call in, now and then, to see to the pump as they wander about in the bush looking for birds and animals. They have been seen far from here too, on the upper part of the Marngu River, beyond into the hills and almost to the end of the Galpu country. Whatever fun there might be in the trapping, the captured wallaby and little joey can bring no joy to the whites. These animals are not like cockatoos to be kept in cages; they will never learn to say a single word to man, and would rather die of hunger than take food from a white hand.

The pump is silent now but it can be very noisy, especially when the wind blows this way, and the rattling of metal bounces against the rock shelter to echo through the bush. The clanking used to be heard even during the night, sucking away not only the water but also the birds and animals that fled in fear. It made Midinari so angry that once he grabbed an ax and wrecked a part of the metal beast, which went suddenly silent—but only for a while.

A small flock of *margu,* flying foxes, swoops around the treetops, sending their shrill squeaks to rebound from the rocks and from the dry bed of the billabong. I have never seen flying foxes around here before, though they are common enough farther down toward the mouth of the Marngu River, in Reyun Country. Clusters of them hang in the mangrove forest that lies along the coast beyond Mount Djangau, and though they have good strong wings and often set out on long journeys, I'm surprised that there's tucker enough to bring them out here. There are hardly any berries left in the bush around here. Maybe the *margu* have been chased out from the mangroves, for the whites are everywhere at Reyun, spreading through the country like ants, digging out soil and rocks and dragging it all far away across the sea.

"Hey, steady on there, little boy. Don't hurt your old mother. Here, I will sit down and keep still for a moment. Is that better?"

Whichever shape one of us is given to live with, be it bird or animal or human, a certain instinct remains by which we can tell when we are not wanted and must move so as not to be trampled. When freed from jail, Midinari moved away from here, to the hills in the farthest upper reaches of the river, and would probably have taken us beyond the horizon if there were a piece of our land there on which to camp. I won't tell him about that wallaby in the trap. It would make him unhappy, and though his anger hides like a red glow in the ashes, it could flare up at the whites at any time. They really got at Midinari in jail. They pinned him to the ground, he said, and . . . he looked as if a bulldozer or one of those great earth-moving machines had rolled over him—such deep scars on his face could hardly have been made by anything else. Perhaps they really meant to finish Midinari off. They couldn't know that my *wawa*, my brother Ruria, would help him and go looking for the *marngit*. That medicine man chanted for days, and with his *dal,* his magic, and the help of the spirit world Midinari's face healed, except . . . there is still that patch where an eye used to be. It no longer bleeds, but it is an angry red and often weeps, attracting flies that cluster and crawl around the hole to lay their maggots in the tender skin.

One of the *margu* is clinging with its finger-like claws to the hanging rock above the shelter and watches me making the fire. It tilts its head now and then, following every move I make, though the dark has almost fallen and all *margu* should be out searching for food and not lingering in the shelter. I must move gently so as not to startle it, for flying foxes are *marain* to all Reyun people. How happy I should be to see the friendly creatures in the Galpu country, but there are no mangrove or pandanus groves for them to hang in during the day and away from the sun, and there is no food.

The whites go to that part of the country but seldom; their tortured cars, sidling between the rocks and crawling over the slopes, whine like ill-treated animals, and the metallic sound travels ahead of them across the country. They come to look for *urban,* emu chicks, and always make a show of asking Midinari's permission to catch the birds in his tribal country, but whenever they call, the old man sits quite still and closes his one remaining eye. It's always the same. The white men stand around for a while peering into Midinari's quiet, scarred face and then decide that his silence means "yes," so they empty their bag on the ground. A pile of treasure lies there—tins of drink, tobacco and matches, barley sugar and biscuits—but Midinari . . . he would not open his eye even if a whole

mountain of white man's nonsense were dumped in front of him. The flies buzz around Midinari's face and cling to the red patch of his wound, but he lifts no hand, even to drive the filthy insects off. The white men walk away to their car and whistle for me to climb on board and show them the tracks through the country. Every time it happens like that—just the same—and Midinari does not move.

The clouds are thick on the far horizon, from one edge of the country to the other, but it will take them a long time to move away from the sea and mass across the burning sky. The sun is already trapped in mist, from which a single ray has escaped to point out a place beyond the distant mangrove forest. There, when the day ends, the sun will plunge into the sea and camp for another night. Mount Djangau should show up in front of the faraway cloud . . . I wonder why I can't see it. That mountain was set down in this country by our first ancestor, who came from the far sea to shape the land and tell our men how to live on it. He made the mountain so tall, with its peak poking into the white belly of the cloud, that it can be seen for miles around by Reyun and Galpu people alike. A man can tell, by looking at that mountain, exactly where he is, so he can never wander to any other place.

The Wet will come soon. Not today or tomorrow—but soon. First will come a great downpour, and then the clouds will settle low, filling the sky for many moons and soaking the soil and the rocks with rain to bring new life to the country, but . . . some of this ruined land could not be brought to life again even if it rained for years. See? A whole part of the country has been stripped almost bare, from here as far as the eye can take you and probably even beyond. There's scarcely a tree left standing. Down at the lower part of the Marngu River . . . well, there's no river there any longer, just hills of bare raw earth, freshly dug and red. The elders say that the earth has blood and guts just as we humans and the other creatures have; but the white men either don't know that, or else don't care. With their huge machines they gallop around the country, ripping it open like an immense carcass with a belly full of red ochre. Huge boulders lie scattered here and there across the bare country, for though the whites have dug the soil and dragged it away, leaving the country behind looking like a dry seabed, the great rocks are nuts too tough for even those metal beasts to crack. A blast here and there knocks off a chunk or two, and the marks of giant metal teeth are sometimes left to scar the rock surface, but still the boulders hold their ground. Strewn, exposed across the country, they might be a flock of turtles from the time before our ancestors, turned into rocks by the spirits. Yes . . . if this country ever comes to life again, *marngit* will have to sing a mighty chant to heal such terrible wounds.

The swarm of *margu* is back again, flying so low that I can feel their wings flapping just above my head and screeching like a mob of children left without tucker for days. They should not have been out in the daytime—they hunt for food only at night, but maybe they cannot sleep with empty bellies. There are no berry bushes left and the mangrove swamp that stretched toward the sea has gone, so anything wishing to survive here now had better learn how to live on rocks and dust. The little *yudu* is getting moody again. How he can kick! Walking on this rough ground covered with loose soil and rocks is tricky. Dust has gathered in the deeper holes and I find them only when my foot plunges. I must stop for a while and lean on that boulder to catch my breath. "Steady, steady little boy; that hurts, that sharp kick. It was not I who made this country so rough. Did I say that I thought of a name for you? Ruria. That should sound nice, and my *wawa* is called that. He is the best tracker in the whole country, you know; even the whites think so. I dreamed about him last night. He was somewhere here in this naked country and had a *ganinjari,* a digging stick, like the one that our first man, Djangau, had when he came, bringing life to the country. Djangau helped the plants to come to life, and Ruria was trying, in my dream, to do the same, but the ground was too rocky and hard and both his palms became blistered. He managed to scratch a hole here and there though, and from each sprang a tiny *marin*, cabbage palm. But the plants were sickly, as though they had germinated out of season and in the wrong soil. The tiny fronds, as yellow as the moon, drooped and grew dry, until there was nothing left of the *marin* but a patch of withered green from which the sun had soaked up the last bit of life.

"This is no place for us now, little Ruria; this valley that was always green and full of shade will never be seen that way again, except in our dreams. Then we will see once more how lovely it was and how dear, not only to man but to the spirits as well."

The Marngu River used to wander through the low part of this country like a snake, leaving a trail of tall trees and deep pools of dark water. The branches stooped and dreamed above these mirrors, admiring their leaves and flowers reflected on the still surface of the water. There was a huge tree just over there . . . no, farther up . . . by that rock. The tree was quite hollow inside, and halfway up the trunk a rotten branch had left an opening where a swarm of bees forever hurried in and out of their home. "You'll see it too, my boy, but not here . . . no . . . but the spirits will show you, in your dreams. Don't you say anything about it to the whites though, will you? They're a cranky lot if they think you know something they don't."

I wonder if Ruria, my brother, is out of jail yet; so many seasons have gone by since they put him there in the lock-up. The last time I came to the hospital I called to see him, but the sergeant was very impatient and would not let me speak with Ruria more than a moment or two. "Come on, hurry up—you'll soon have him back, and all your precious country as well—the bloody lot." The white man was sneering, laughing. It didn't seem strange then, but now. . . .

They should have set Ruria free long ago; he had done no harm. He let poor Midinari out, certainly, but the old man was already a harmless ruin. I don't see why it made the sergeant so angry that he should put my *wawa* in the lock-up instead, and keep him there so long; and all in spite of Ruria's good work tracking day and night across the country, hunting men and dingoes for the whites.

"Hold on there, little man. That hurts." We should stop and camp here, for darkness is falling already; only the tops of the boulders can be seen, with deep shadow between. Let's lie down here in the dust and curl up for the night, though the noisy *margu* flapping and crying in the dark will keep me awake for a while, I reckon. When Ruria comes out of jail the country will be no easier on him unless . . . maybe the whites will have taught him how to survive by eating rocks. When I see him this time I will tell him that he must come to us. Galpu is still a big country, though only the far end, the hilly part, is left to us, its true people. Midinari will be glad to have Ruria around, I'm sure.

The boy has gone to sleep. I must not stir or breathe too deeply in case I disturb him. This must be the last *yudu;* Purelko, Lanygara, Urbudal, Ngadu, Dugar, Eanibugei, and now Ruria—but if my *wawa* comes to live with us, he can tell the white men in their own lingo, when they come with their car again, that no *urban* live in our part of the country. He can say that the hills are too steep for emus and that hardly any seeds or berries grow there, and I will not have to go with the white men any more. They can take back the tins, the old clothes, the tea . . . they will not need to open the bag. We will make *ganinjari* again—Midinari can do that with his stone ax, as the men did in the old time—and I will wander in the bush, scratching the earth until I have gathered a bagful of roots and grasses. We will survive on whatever the land is kind enough to give us.

A willy-willy swirls across the empty stretch of bare earth ahead, whirling a huge column of dust skyward and dashing it . . . but look—Mount Djangau has gone! There's nothing—nothing but an empty space. It's as though a chunk of the sky as well as the land had been snatched away to open the view to the country lying behind. A jumble of boulders, large and small, are left behind—just a crumb of the hill that has pushed upward into the mist since the day the spirits set it there. A whole mountain cannot just shrink—no, rocks are too tough for that. So . . . the whites must have done this thing. Have they dragged it right across the sea to their own country? They might wish to make a new mountain for themselves there, but no . . . I think Midinari and the other men are right; the whites are taking the rocks to pound them into dust. Is their land without dust, then? I must not say anything of this; it will make Midinari angry, and . . . his time is short. The spirits will tell him soon enough what happened to the country, and they will tell it better than I.

"Hey, steady there, steady on, my boy. It won't be long now. Look, the hospital is hardly a voice or two away."

There seems to be no one about; perhaps the whites are having a snooze after a good lunch, or maybe they've gone down to the shore of the bay, hoping for a breeze to come from the open sea. The sun makes the white men suffer—turns their light skins red, makes them pant and sweat—but they seem unable to learn from the animals not to rush about in the heat. They should hide during the day in shady corners, and only come out at dusk and dawn, when the air around is cool and kind.

Don't get so wild with me, young Ruria. Just wait a little and the nurse will smile at you, give you a nice cot to rest on, feed you . . . and when you've grown a bit she will give you barley sugar and sweet drinks. They keep boxes of Coca-Cola at the hospital, you know."

I wonder if they let my *wawa* out to catch some of the sea breeze; that jail hut made of tin and heavy wire mesh must be like a boiling billy. Surely they would let him out now and then to catch his breath—even if only to make sure that his life does not come to an end.

"Be patient, my boy. All the other *yudu* are near—Purelko, Lanygara, Urbudal, Ngadu, Dugar, and Eanibugei, and though the whites might call them different names, their skin will keep the shadow of their ancestors and yours. They are your brothers and sisters—whatever the white man calls them."

What's this? The jail hut is gone, the spear grass has grown tall in the empty compound, and an old blanket, flung there by the willy-willy, flaps from the top of the barbed-wire fence. Beyond, fringing the bay, there should be a row of huts, half hidden in the shade . . . but what is left? A post or two, a few corrugated iron sheets, a pile of bottles, and a great stain on the ground—nothing more.

A flock of *margu* swoops out through a shattered window of the hospital, but one, dazzled perhaps by reflected sunlight, is impaled, struggling on broken glass. At last it falls to the grass outside, its wings fluttering like torn rags and leaving behind a trail of blood and the dry smell of dust.

The squealing of a wounded soul is heard for a time, but presently all is quiet, the dust settles, and the blood becomes caked and hard in the bright sun.

Five-dog Night

How could a soul live in a cage made like a compound? In Pitjanta, my tribal country, we have the whole bush to roam in, but here, whichever way you turn, a wire mesh meets your face. A whole pack of us is locked inside the enclosure—every color and shape. If the whites do not finish me soon I will be torn apart by these wild mongrels.

The whites are up to something; both the warden and his boss are here. They point through the mesh at me. Perhaps they're not happy at seeing me still around. Every day the small shutter at the end of the compound is raised, letting out a bunch of inmates: they run along a short passage until they reach a bunker. Soon after, a puff of smoke rises from a chimney and the smell of charcoaled flesh lingers in the air. Why do those mongrels enter that oven? Perhaps they know the end awaits them in there, but . . . is there anything better worth waiting for here?

Warden has come inside. He waves his dog-catching gadget and slides the noose over my head. I'd better not struggle no matter where he takes me. I could have headed into that bunker days ago, but I do not wish my ashes to be scattered over the town and the green paddocks beyond—so far from Pitjanta I might never find my way back to our own world, or see Wati, my old master, again.

The noose tightens around my neck, and Warden jerks me forward: "C'mon out, we don't want any trouble here."

An Alsatian snaps at my back; other dogs rush too. A poodle clings with his feet to the tip of my tail and swings, trying to drag me back. Lucky I am being taken away. If I stayed in the compound and grew too weak to fight back, the savage beasts would tear me open. The day the whites threw me in, I saw one of our fellows; he must have been taken from the bush long before, from the signs of a worn collar and tag, and had grown old and blind. The other dogs ganged up against him; like humans, animals can smell the bush and tell a different blood. . . . Poor, blind fellow—a few whiskers and the metal number tag was the little left over.

"We're going to make it up to you."

Warden must remember me from the time he spent in Pitjanta. He had been in the bush for years and had run a small compound in the settlement—an enclosure fenced in much the same as the one here, though there he had kept Wati and other tribal fellows inside. Perhaps the white man now feels sorry to see me go into that oven and will hang me instead, letting my soul return to the bush to join our mob. Wati, my old master, needs to be kept warm at night wherever he might be; I should be there to snuggle into him as the cold creeps in at dawn.

This noose is choking me. I could pry it looser if I could stick my claws into it while not being dragged forward. Warden rushes through a door inside the building. Why must they put me on the scales?—they have never measured a dog before. Besides, whatever one's weight, here it ends in the same way: a handful of ashes. Maybe they plan to butcher me—food for those mongrels. Warden says little, though he glances at his boss: "Doctor, he could do with a few more kilos. . . ."

"Shouldn't you clap a muzzle on his snout?" The boss wears a white coat; he has a trimmed beard and a pair of spectacles over his eyes.

"Old dingoes grow wise; they're like those Abo elders—no struggle."

Wati was like that. He hardly yelled or cursed, just sat on the ground of the compound, chained to a dry gum tree, chanting now and then. The buzzing of flies and the hot sun drowned his voice during the day, but by evening the chanting floated through the air, angering Warden. Often the white man would rush from his hut, and grabbing the loose end of the chain, swing it against Wati's face. Perhaps he feared the chant was a call for our tribal fellows to emerge with spears and storm the settlement.

Warden smiles now: "What a fine bristly tail you have here. I'll give you a good brush later."

On the settlement that same white face had always looked gloomy, though I never got too close. It was always dark when I sneaked away from the bush, climbing over the chain-wire fence and tiptoeing across the sandy ground of the compound. No light was needed to show the way to the master. You simply raised your snout, caught a breath of air, then followed the lead. I could not fully see Wati's face then, but beneath my tongue it felt like *kampura*—a wild tomato—that someone had stepped on. Wounds heal quickly when you lick them, washing away sand and dirt and the stuff the flies leave behind to become maggots. I even mopped up blood that had run into the bushy beard.

"We have to be absolutely sure"—the eyes behind the spectacles glanced at me.

"When we were in the bush he slept with his old man. I saw him every morning getting over the fence from the compound. He's the only Pitjanta soul left. Look at his face, Doc, the bastard knows me."

"A descendant, you mean," corrected the white-coated man.

"Yes, he's one of the Abos all right."

"Smarten him up a bit."

The bespectacled man might be my new master. I will have to hug him during the night as I did Wati. Nights were cold in the compound; that dry gum tree gave no shelter. We scratched a hole in the sandy ground, but not deep enough to keep us properly warm. A corrugated iron sheet to make a windbreak would have helped, even a branch or two might have brought a good night's rest, but nothing came our way. In his sleep Wati always chanted, whispering to our *tjamus*—spirits—urging them to fetch him from the compound, but they never came. Perhaps the nights were too cold for our spirits to be abroad, or the chant may have been too weak to stir them.

The whites seem to be trying to make amends for past cruelties; I have been given a warm blanket to cover me. Around me is a cage with enough room to stretch in but no space for running. Still, I could prop up against the bars. Every day now, Warden gives me a bath, warming the tub of water and dipping me in while he rubs soap harshly over my fur. "You never had it so good," he sneers, rubbing me dry with a towel. "There is more of this to come, wait till you see the lot." The voice of the white man has softened, and he smiles often. He might let me out of the cage soon; this room I'm kept in is large enough for a stroll. I would not try to duck out through the door—too old to run, and why struggle? Soon I shall be off to the black man's world; Wati and every Pitjanta soul are there—only I am kept outside, and . . . it should not be for much longer now.

"Drink your milk, have some dog biscuits." Warden points to two bowls in the cage.

Wati was given a bowl too, though much bigger, almost the size of a bucket. "Catch some water in that when your spookies bring the rain," he was told. The elder knew the right words to summon our *tjamus* to send clouds, but he was never allowed to chant loudly enough to make his call reach our spirit world, and what can a lonely voice do with no tribesmen left to support?

Warden has brought me a tray full of sand and placed it on the cage bottom. "Mess inside when you have to, the way cats do." The white man has taught me how to shake a hand; each morning when he comes in I must prop up, poke out a front paw, and shake his limbs for a while. Humans do that often, though I have never seen dogs greeting each other so. "Wag that tail—I'm your chaperone now. We're stuck together for life."

Today the white man holds his newspaper, spread open, in front of the cage. "Two whole pages about you, my friend." Yes, there is a large picture of me wearing a bow tie on my collar. "Here, let me read it to you. . . . "

They say I am the only survivor of the Pitjanta tribe and that I have been reincarnated from the soul of one of our fellows. The whites believe it at last; in the bush, every dog is black man's relative—reborn in a different shape but still hanging about the camp and seeking to hug humans at night, to keep them warm. Wati knew all about who is related to whom at Pitjanta, not only the humans but all the animals, trees, and stars.

Look, Wati's picture is in the paper too, not photographed like the one of me, but a drawing, blurred in parts and without any scars on his face. Nor are the chains to be seen—however, the trunk of that dead tree they tied him to is there.

"The scientists claim that when chanting he was in fact calling for rain. Rain came, though it is years now, and the whole bush was changed into green paddocks. Your old master has been given the Order of the British Empire, posthumously of course."

I doubt whether Wati will come back, whatever the whites lure him with. His spirit still wanders in the bush and beckons me in dreams to follow him. The nights may be cold in that spirit world just as they are in the bush—and when you grow old you feel the cold easily.

"Let me clip your claws. We'll be seeing the governor today; they'll pin a medal on your collar; you're the only descendant of Wati's that we can trace."

Pity they took me out away from the compound. I could have

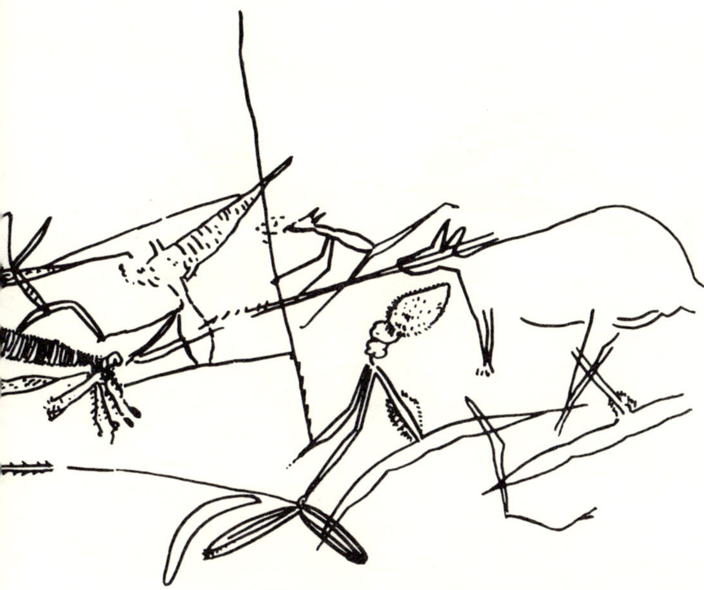

been on the way to my people by now. Wati used to shiver in his sleep, and often muttered "five-dog night"—that is how many of us were needed to keep one man warm.

A tip of claw nail flies up as it is snipped off. "Tomorrow the doctor will present you to a symposium of R.A.S.P.,* then he'll be off to show you to the rest of the world."

Warden's hand reaches for my head, to scratch behind my ears. I should snap off his finger—that will keep him away, maybe for good!

The white face leans forward, a red, swollen nose passing between the bars of the cage. "Doc hopes to turn you into a human again—a white this time. I shall have to teach you how to handle a spoon."

No, I'd better not snap at that face, but leave without a struggle, as my old man did. My body has begun to shrink already, and if I don't eat for two more days, that will see me off and . . . I don't think the whites will notice. They will curse their luck once I am gone to Wati, but that will not bring any of us back.

* Royal Academy of Science and Progress.

The Billabong

An evil spell must have caught up with Ranger. He called on me last night and cursed: "They're out to get me! Drive the devils off, hurry!"

It takes a long while for man or spirit to come down from Mount Wawalag, cross the wide swampy plain and go far beyond it, almost to the edge of the horizon where the land meets the sea, and reach the cliff at last. That is about half of Gamitj, our country. What a pity Ranger does not live closer—by the time I reach him we could have eaten the biggest barrimundi and grown hungry again.

The sun is racing to the noon; however hot the day grows it will not make me break my journey, though. It is lucky for Ranger and me that there are so many trees about here—you can walk from one shade to another all the way across the plain. The paperbarks grow tall out here—the top branches are tucked under the armpit of the sky to shield us from the heat.

One of my knees has gone numb—going too fast perhaps. I had better stop to catch my breath, lean on one of the paperbarks for a while, but not sit down, for I can easily doze off on a hot day like this. Some of those trees have grown so tall—to stretch any farther they will have to push up the blue canopy of the sky. What a pity Ranger is not here. He likes to pat the trunks of the paperbarks and say: "Each of them is one of our fellows—there are more trees around here than all the living black and white souls put together."

Wind lashes the top branches and they sway, letting the sun into the shady forest. How will the trees feel if Ranger goes? They need him, not so much perhaps as they need the sun and the air, but to grow it helps to have someone around who will pat you now and then. The white man did not tell me much about the curse that has struck him, but someone is after him for sure: "Keep those bloody spookies away from me—you're *marngit* after all," he told me in the dream.

I have to press on with the journey; about a voice or two away the track will come to Birany, a large billabong, and then follow the edge of the water all the way to the cliff. I will move much faster once I have quenched my thirst. Ranger will hold on, he has been in trouble before—yes, a snake bit him many monsoons ago. Baba, my father, was around then; he raced up Mount Wawalag almost puffing out his old soul: "Come down and heal him—that man harms neither us nor the country."

Though he is white, Ranger must have been around in the bush most of his life. You can tell by the way he handles the *dudji,* spinning one of them between his palms, pressing the other one between his knees against the ground. When it flames up he throws on only a few branches and lets them glow steadily—you can always tell if a man is used to the bush by how big a fire he makes.

The water tastes warm; I had better not drink too much—a full belly slows you down. Ranger will have his billy boiling when I reach his hut at the cliff; he never fails to give me tea. In his Land Rover he carries all that is necessary to make a good drink—cups, sugar, and a box of biscuits. Smoke lingering among the branches always tells me when he is about. I am not sure if he lit the fire to lure me down from the mountain or to make a hot drink for himself. It could be both—he never fails to welcome me: "Have as many lumps of sugar as you like," he always tells me as we sip cup after cup from a blackened billy. Last night his voice sounded different, scared stiff: "Hurry here, they're tossing me into the estuary!"

The cliff cannot be seen yet but should appear soon. You do not have to worry if you are on the right track; just follow the edge of the forest where the trees lean over the still water of Birany—the billabong stretches farther than the eye can reach and is a good day's journey wide for those of us who can make it across the water. Seen from the mountain, it looks like an eel that has crawled out of the water and is lying on the plain, stretched almost to the foot of Mount Wawalag. Why does the white man call it "estuary"?

Hold on for a while—my knee feels funny. On the way back to the hills I will look for some goanna fat to rub on it and bury my poor leg in hot sand—that often brings life back to a limb, whatever it might be suffering from. I shall ask Ranger to move closer—there are many high places on the plain that are safe from floods where he can put his hut. Baba tried to talk him into that too. The two of them were great friends—the white man always carried packs of tobacco and they often sat in the shade of a banyan tree the whole day, puffing smoke. Ranger was given a Macassan pipe by my father; it had a crocodile—our totem—carved on it, just like the one the old man made for himself.

The heat of the day is making me doze off; I have to splash some water over my face, that will help. You do not go into the water here. Ranger too has learned to stay away from the billabong; when he feels like swimming he looks for some other pool. Birany is not sacred to him too, but the white man would not upset *baru,* the crocodiles—they are his totem also. He even carries one of them painted on his chest, just as the old men do when they dress up for a ceremony, though the animal never seems to wash off the white skin. Perhaps Ranger was born with his *baru,* or some of our spirits did him a special favor and made the picture of the reptile grow into his skin.

The water is murky today; it usually looks like that only during floods, though the monsoon is not here yet. It could be a whole moon till the rains come. Before they do, a boat will call in—you see it coming from Mount Wawalag when the weather is fine, a turtle beating its way to the shore.

I have never seen the boat when it is anchored against the cliff. The vessel looks small when seen from a distance, but my father says it is bigger than Ranger's hut on the cliff. It has the shape of a swollen belly and can carry piles of sugar bags, tea, and tins of food. Ranger's Land Rover rode on the boat too, and so did his large canoe, to take him around our country in the floods during the Wet. When the boat was here last he asked me to come and see it, and that did not please Baba: "You stay up on Mount Wawalag, that is *marngit*'s place." Not long after, when he was passing away, I was told again: "Hold onto our world."

If I press hard on the journey I can reach the cliff by evening. Ranger will have to hold on until then, whatever trouble might have struck him. Perhaps he . . . yes, the boat might have come in, and to lure me there the white man is pretending to be ill. It might not be right for a medicine man to go on the boat—that thing floats and goes fast; before you notice it you could be taken to the open sea, and what would Gamitj country do without me, the healer, then?

I have to climb down the bank and drink again. The water has ebbed away from the roots—I can hold onto them with one hand and lean down to plunge the other into Birany. When you lean out above the pool to drink you have to be quick; *baru* do not like us coming close to the water—the billabong is their home and you often see them sunbathing on the bank or wallowing in the mud. None of them have come out today, though they will not be far away; crocodiles often peep from under lily pads with only a snout and a pair of eyes poking out, silently tracking whoever is about to plunge into the water, ready to strike angrily at him.

The billabong must have been murky for days: a layer of mud has covered the lily pads. The silt will anger Baba, for he is down in the water too. When a Gamitj man dies his soul goes into Birany and becomes a crocodile. A full tribe of our fellows is down there—the billabong is their home now, and sacred to us all. Ranger, too, keeps away from the water, though he can enter the billabong through a short channel from the tidal river near the cliff. I saw him once, dragging a buffalo carcass to the edge of the billabong and throwing the animal to a crocodile: "Your Baba was a good man, let him have a whole beast."

The cliff is visible at last—a good way off, though. There should be a flag there flapping in the breeze. The white man must have felt too ill to raise it this morning. Before, when he was suffering from that snakebite, Baba raised it for him, and he did it too quickly so the rope got knotted. I had to climb up the pole to free the flag and then came down a bit fast—yes, that was when I hurt my poor knee.

I shall tell Ranger that the water is murky—he might do something about it. The white man often tells me: "You look after people; I care for trees and animals—Gamitj country never had it so good." When he arrived in the bush he had a hard time learning to say "Birany" and he called the billabong "estuary," the same name he uses for the river. Baba did not like it; the two men often sat in the shade of the banyan tree looking at the still water covered with lily pads, each repeating his own word for it. It is good that it has dawned on Ranger at last that the billabong is not just a stretch of stagnant water but a place we will all come to at the end. He will come with us too—crocodiles do not sit in the shade or smoke pipes but he and Baba will sunbathe together and swap news about good wallowing places.

Hold on, someone has been around here—footprints on the sand lead into the billabong. It could not have been Ranger, his boots have a honeycomb pattern, but these—they look plain. Whoever was here has dragged something out of the water and headed back into the bush. On my way back I will follow the track. The white man has to be told of this; he will be out here as quick as a storm to chase the intruder away, even if he has to crawl after him: "The bush is totem for us all—tell me if anyone harms it," he often says.

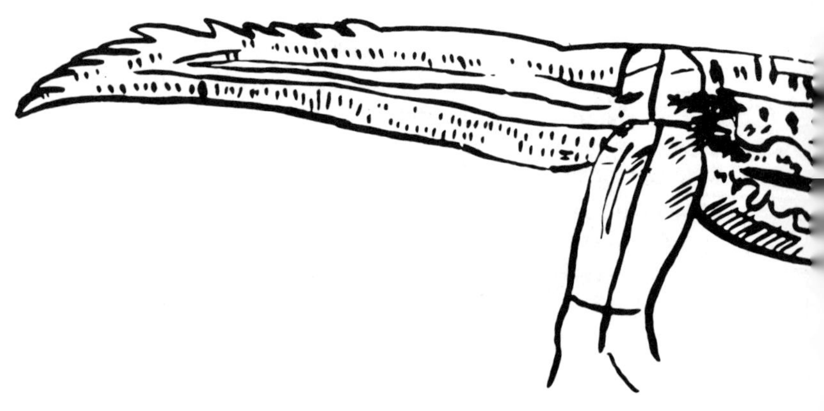

What a pity Ranger does not live here in the bush to keep an eye on the billabong; raising that flag on the cliff does not do much good for us or the crocodiles. How many of them has the hunter dragged out of the water? Last time someone sneaked in, Baba was with us, and though he is old he tracks better than any other fellow—no man can get away unless he flies or goes out to sea. The last hunters were tracked across the river and the country beyond—Baba did not want to give up the chase but he was told: "The white man's law will catch the thieves." The boards with the white man's lingo were nailed on tree trunks along the river banks to warn the hunters to keep off Baba Reserve.

It is a pity the Reserve is named after my father—Ranger wanted it that way and no man or spirit could persuade him otherwise. Had it been called Birany, that would have been a word that is so much more than just the name of a man—it means a whole world, sacred to Gamitj people and every black soul. The people, black and white alike, will stay away from the billabong, fearing that the spirits of the dead will chase them until the ends of their lives if they disturb the sacred place.

My poor, troubled leg—I had better sit for a while and rub it. The rest should do me good. Look, there is a net draped over the lily pads. Perhaps . . . yes, it must have been placed farther down across that channel leading to the river. There was a windstorm last night and it has drifted up here. Ranger will have to move his hut here. Yes, he likes to eat lobsters and wants to be closer to the sea, but I have to make him move. If the hunters are allowed to get away with the loot they will be back. Baba and every one of us could end up in that net waiting to be skinned when we die.

An arm of the billabong has dried up and the bare, muddy ground has hardened. Yes, I can take a shortcut across that stretch and be quicker. There is no smoke or flag to be seen from the cliff. Some bad thing must indeed have caught up with Ranger. The trees might not like it if he goes, for there will be no one left to pat them. Another white man might come and keep an eye on the bush. Would he throw a buffalo into the billabong as well? The crocodiles like to be cared for too. Why did Baba never ask about Ranger? He often calls into my dreams and talks to me about the country and all the tribal souls, but never a word about the white man. The crocodiles might know much more about Ranger than the humans do and not be pleased. No, I could never go onto the boat; we have our world to hold onto, as Baba said.

What has happened to the white man's hut? You should be able to see it from here. Baba told me that when a strong storm comes one day it will toss that hut down into the river. No man builds his shelter on top of a cliff. Why did he not talk about Ranger any more? I doubt if he liked the white man being boss of Gamitj country and caring for our trees. If Baba had had any say he would have named a black man to do that or, better still, have left the country to the tribal elders and me, *marngit*—who else knows more about the bush than we do?

Two large trees have been uprooted and one of them tossed into the billabong about half a voice away from the bank. There must have been quite a storm here, though hardly any of it reached Mount Wawalag. The storms always come from the sea and lash against the coast after the long race over the sea; then they wear themselves out after knocking down some trees here and there. Only the storms coming during the monsoon are strong enough to reach inland to the mountain.

Where will Ranger store his supplies if the hut is blown away? The boat does not come often and the load that arrives soon will have to see him through the Wet. He might have to build a new hut from saplings and cover it with tree bark. What a pity Baba is not here; he promised the white man that he would make him one in return for a steel ax, but after waiting for so many years to be told where the hut should be erected, the old soul left without returning the favor.

It must have been a night of anger and curses when the storm hit the cliff. The wind uprooted the banyan tree and the branches flattened the hut. Several corrugated iron panels must have come loose earlier and flown off toward the river. One of them hit the crown of a paperbark, took off a few branches, and stuck among the top limbs of the tree.

Racks of crocodile hides lie hidden amidst the crushed timber and twisted metal of the hut—so many of them, dried and tightly packed so as not to come apart during the long journey. What do the whites need them for? Crocodiles have no fur to make rugs from, and if you ever try to rest on one of them, the spirit of the dead beast will creep onto you.

Some of the skins have fallen off one of the piles and are scattered around in the bush. One of them is stuck on the flagpole and sways in the wind, tangled in the ropes. I must climb up and bring it down, then gather the rest of the skins and take them down to the billabong. Ranger must have gone down to the water too; neither he nor his track is to be seen. He will have to explain it all to the crocodiles or . . . yes, the beasts already know all about it—those buffalo joints were only bait.

The breeze blows up and flaps the skin on the pole. I doubt if the boat will ever come to the cliff again. The whites would not like to come so far with sacks of sugar and tea, and steel axes, if there is no loot to be taken away. It is a pity they did not make a black man the ranger or leave Gamitj country to us to care for.

Wirgul, the Daughter

Do the whites know much about the shape we live in? Good if they do not, for I am changed into an emu. My size has not shrunk, though, and I still have two long legs and a rumbling, nervous belly. As for clothes, feathers are thick and warm. My neck has been stretched out—it feels like a thick vine swaying about with a head on top.

Is Baba, my father, angry that I am not a girl any longer? He says nothing and I doubt if he will ever complain. The blind never talk about how others look, and I had better not cluck too much and annoy him. "Let's play again." He wets his lips with his tongue, then places a gum leaf between them—and blows a tune.

I have to accompany the sound of the leaf with the clattering of my beak. The noise I make lags behind him; I have to be careful that my tongue is not caught by my beak. Before, when I had human shape, I had *bilma,* the clapping sticks—quite an old pair given to Baba by a tribal elder. The sticks must have been old: when you held them each finger rested in a depression worn by human touch. What a pity I will never be able to hold them again. Let us hope the clattering of my beak will make a sound close enough to the *bilma* and not anger my father. Whatever has happened to my shape, I am still *wirgul,* his daughter.

A coin hits the bowl, jingling as it comes to rest in the bottom of the empty container. Baba never misses a bow to a passerby as soon as he hears the sound of a coin. I used to bow and smile too, though that is not expected of me now.

"Look, the Apostle has gone pop!" It is a bunch of young whites who pass along the pavement about noon every day and throw a button or two into the bowl, never a coin. Yesterday they asked Baba to show them how to play the leaf. They will never learn—the gum trees here grow differently from those at Djabu, our tribal country, and the leaves are not the same—even poor Father has to struggle to make the sound come through in a tune that will please the whites.

A lad throws an apple core into the bowl: "Apostle, make her do a belly dance—she'll freeze on that concrete if she stays still."

Yes, it feels very cold. Luckily I have a thick feather cover to keep my body warm and Baba has a worn blanket over his shoulders, though it hardly seems to help much. His lips have grown blue and his eyes are both weeping. Snow has fallen—not here, but the hills beyond the town look this morning as though someone has covered them with cockatoo feathers.

Baba stops blowing into the leaf, wipes his weeping, milky eyes, and hurries to tuck his shivering hand under the blanket. He knows there is snow about; he must have learned that earlier in the morning as soon as we crawled out from under our shelter. He jigged for a while, running on a nature strip by the road and whispering: "Don't worry, snow never falls in town."

How long does winter last here? Perhaps it stays longer than the Wet does up in the bush we come from. He has not told me yet why snow falls and not monsoon rain—perhaps the whites prefer to see the hills above the town a bright color. When he was in our country Baba hardly ever mentioned snow and never spoke of the town either. Every Djabu soul knows he came from the white man's world but stayed in the bush for too long, eating sweet potatoes cooked in hot ashes, and his skin grew darker like ours. The white man's spirit boss was angry with him for mixing with us and brought about the curse: "Bloody trachoma" Baba calls it.

Several more coins hit the bowl—a group of people have gathered to watch me clapping my beak. I had better not raise my head too high, the whites might be frightened of being pecked. Have they ever seen an emu before?—perhaps the bird only lives in the bush. All the better—those hills covered with snow might look pretty and bright but no one eats that icy stuff.

The people want to take a picture—I have to move closer to Baba and lean my long neck against his arm while we perform. His voice has gone dry and his body shrunk—he must hate the snow too. If you live in a warm country and sleep under a tree for a good part of your life, a town will look odd whatever color your skin might be.

The whites have packed their cameras, but before they leave each of them pulls some feathers out of me. I do not mind giving a quill or two, but it feels very cold today and I would rather not part with too many. A hand from the crowd reaches for my back—a few more grabs like that and only goose pimples will be left behind on my skin. I should hide behind Baba when the whites are around—pass my head under his arm and clatter my beak. Father will surely shield me; he has been nice to birds ever since he came to Djabu country and stretched his hammock under a banyan tree. Whenever he took cooked *muwugu* from the hot ashes a piece was always put aside. A pair of *wanba,* pigeons, often perched on the lower branches waiting to be called by the sound of his gum leaf, and then they would fly down to land on his arm and pick at the food.

One of the passersby handed out what looked to be a piece of barley sugar, but it tasted . . . it was the butt of a burning cigarette that they tucked into my beak! I must not complain; Baba has enough worries already and his few remaining teeth rattle loudly. Is it fear or the cold that makes his jaws chatter? I wish we had never come to town—the bush made him much happier. The tribal elders liked him being around—perhaps for feeding *wanba,* our totem—and he was given a young woman to make him campfires and cook. His hammock lasted for several Wets, and when it rotted he did not go to look for another one but dug a pit in the ground for us all to curl up in during cold nights, just as every black family does.

"We'll go back to the bush soon." Baba tucks his hands under my feathers to keep them warm. His teeth sound even louder now—a pair of pebbles rattling in an empty dish. What a pity Mother is not with us; she knew how to make him well. When we were in the bush and the weather turned cold she always baked *ngadu,* a big damper, in the hot ashes. He held the steaming hot food close to his face: "It smells as sweet as nectar." Damper

sometimes tastes bitter if the cycad nuts it was made from have not been properly soaked in water, but it was the warmth, not the food, that mattered.

Ouch! My poor feathers! A passerby has pulled out a whole handful of them. A patch of skin on my back is already bald, and the drafts of cold wind freeze the tender skin. If I was in Djabu I would fight back; here, I would not even pick on a jellyfish!

No coin has hit the bowl for a while. The gum leaf might not sound so mellow to white ears as before, or . . . the people could have been put off by my clattering. I doubt if the bowl will ever be full; that might not matter any more, though. Yesterday Baba said that a whole bag full of coins would be needed to pay the white medicine man to get rid of the trachoma spell. What a pity Marngit could not help. . . . He asked for no coins, and felt too shy to take even a piece of damper wrapped in banana leaves Mother took to him: "It's the white man's curse, not ours," he told her. The medicine man chanted for days and said that if his eyes did not take a turn for the better, Father should beg the white man's spirit boss to be relieved from the spell.

Baba sits on the concrete pavement now and leans on me heavily; he is about to say something and still holds his mouth open, but he has dozed off suddenly without a word. One of his cheeks trembles for a moment before that too becomes peaceful. Let him sleep for a while. Last night we camped in a storm-water pipe, drafty and cold. The few teeth in Baba's mouth rattled ceaselessly, only letting out a whispered "Let's head back to the bush tomorrow."

We might be on our way back to Djabu this afternoon. There are enough coins in the bowl for a loaf of bread. It will be a long journey though—our country and the town here are two different worlds, so many camps apart that no black soul could ever count them. Mother once asked Marngit how long one has to journey to reach the white man's healer and was told: "Much longer than our mind can stretch."

One of Baba's hands grips my feathers and then, losing strength, slides down the quills. The skin of his arm has turned ashy-gray, almost concealing the cross tatooed above his wrist. That mark has been with him since before he arrived in our country. He might have been born with it; Mother was told that the cross is the white man's totem. It is good that the tattooed mark is fading. In the bush Father used to curse: "I can do without you here," and angrily he often tried to rub the mark off his arm with sand.

The bunch of youths is back. "Hey, Apostle, let your bird do a belly dance." Why do they call him that strange name? Maybe because of the rubber thongs he wears or the old blanket wrapped around his shoulders. It is good that Baba has dozed off—that nickname makes him mumble. I am not so good at the white man's lingo as to know what they mean, but I feel Father's wounded soul.

One of the boys tickles a bare patch of skin on my back: "Let's have some fun with the nude." Another youth reaches for the bowl; when he has emptied it, he kicks the dish and it rattles along the pavement. Baba says nothing though his face moves. His mouth is open, the corners twitch, but it stops before he can talk. Perhaps . . . yes, all old men must look the same when they depart, whichever world they might be destined to go to.

Two men in white overcoats rush out from a paddy van marked with a red cross. One of them pokes the end of his shoe into Baba's body and says: "The old bugger's kicked the bucket."

Baba's eyes remain open. A white hand forces the eyelids shut but the skin soon springs back, revealing a pair of milky pupils set in dark hollows. The eyelids are pulled down again, only to retreat. The men mumble some angry words and push Baba's body into the paddy van. Perhaps the whites are eager not to let Father see where he is being taken, but he is trying to tell them that once a man is under the trachoma spell the whole world sinks into the dark.

I should find a dark corner to squeeze into for the rest of the day and about dusk head toward the bush. Though our country is so many camps away, emus have a good pair of legs; I will see the end of the track. The spirits of the dead travel much faster than birds—when I reach Djabu, Baba may already have gathered a pile of kindling wood to make a campfire.

Glossary

babaru—family
badi—dilly bag
bala—initiated
balanda—white man
balandja—white cockatoo
bandja—cave
baru—crocodile
bilma—clapping sticks
boong—derogatory term for aborigines
Bralgu—land of the dead
dabalan—caterpillar
dal—magic power
didjeridu—immense, deep-noted wind instrument made from up to eight feet of hollow tree
djojmenu—totemic place
djuwi—spirit, child's spiritual genitor
Dreaming, Dreamtime—myth of creation
dudji—fire-making sticks
dugaruru—sacred stone, ritual emblem for regeneration
duwei—husband, man
galdj—stone ax
galei—woman
ganinjari—digging stick
gin—aboriginal woman
jadara ameri-gamari—like propped goannas
kaltu—seed from wild grass *(Panicum decompositum)*
kampura—wild tomato

kury—wife
lalai—mythical time, totem
lap-lap—cover around waist
larpan—magic spear carried by Thunder Man
lindaridj—galah (pink-breasted cockatoo), parakeet
maba—old man
maidja—breast girdle worn by women
marain—totem, sacred place
margu—flying fox
marin—cabbage palm
marngit—medicine man
mauwulan—walking stick
munga—spirit world (term used in Central Australia)
murlg—shelter, hut
muwugu—sweet potato
nadu, ngadu—damper, made usually of cycad nuts
namanama—tribal country
nara—fertility ceremony
njuga—crab
nura—tribal country (term used in Central Australia)
nyuma—loaf of damper (term used in Central Australia)
piti—wooden dish
ranga—sacred
titi—boy
tjamu—spirit ancestor
urban—emu
walg—womb, uterus, umbilical cord
walu—sun
wanba—pigeon
wardu—malevolent spirit
warngi—monster
wati—tribal elder
wawa—brother
wirgul—young girl
wongar—spirit world (same as Dreaming)
wulun—paperbark tree
yapu—mountain
yudu—child